# THE DOLPHINS' BELL

# ====== THE ====== DOLPHINS' ===== BELL =====

## ANNE McCAFFREY

### Illustrated by PAT MORRISSEY

The Wildside Press
Newark, NJ = 1993

THE DOLPHINS' BELL

Published by The Wildside Press

All Rights Reserved.

No portion of this book may be reproduced by any means, electronic or otherwise, without the express written concent of the author, except for brief passages embodied in critical essays or reviews.

For more information, contact:

The Wildside Press
37 Fillmore Street
Newark, NJ 07105

Book design by John Betancourt

ISBN: 1-880448-33-5 (numbered edition)
ISBN: 1-880448-34-3 (lettered edition)

# ----- THE ----- DOLPHINS' ----- BELL -----

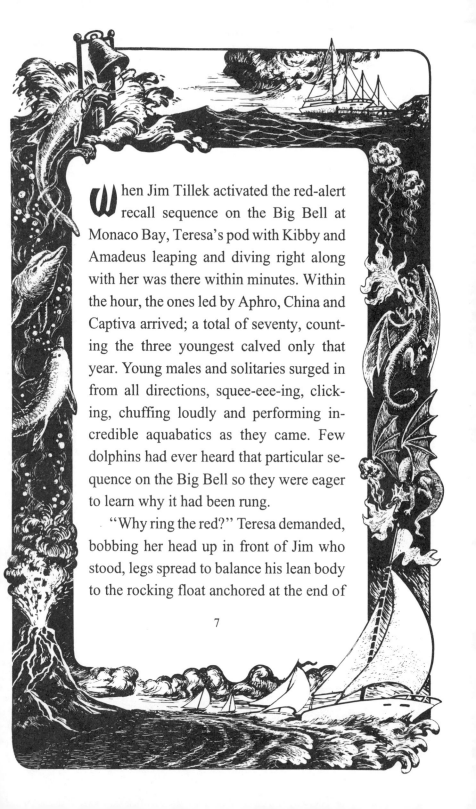

When Jim Tillek activated the red-alert recall sequence on the Big Bell at Monaco Bay, Teresa's pod with Kibby and Amadeus leaping and diving right along with her was there within minutes. Within the hour, the ones led by Aphro, China and Captiva arrived; a total of seventy, counting the three youngest calved only that year. Young males and solitaries surged in from all directions, squee-eee-ing, clicking, chuffing loudly and performing incredible aquabatics as they came. Few dolphins had ever heard that particular sequence on the Big Bell so they were eager to learn why it had been rung.

"Why ring the red?" Teresa demanded, bobbing her head up in front of Jim who stood, legs spread to balance his lean body to the rocking float anchored at the end of

7

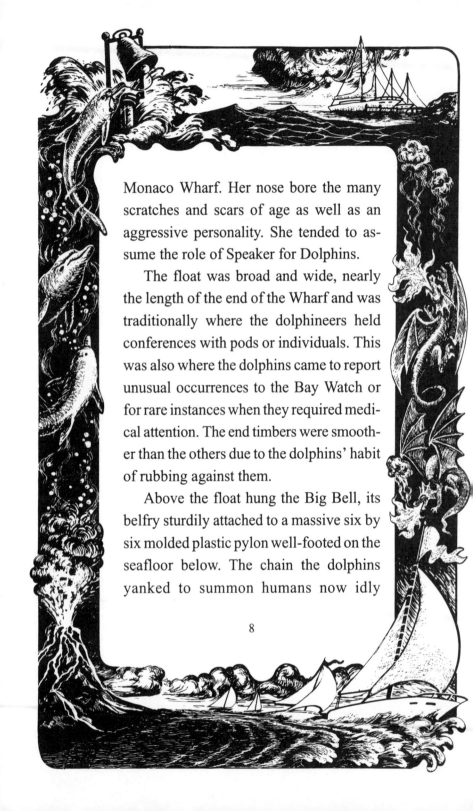

Monaco Wharf. Her nose bore the many scratches and scars of age as well as an aggressive personality. She tended to assume the role of Speaker for Dolphins.

The float was broad and wide, nearly the length of the end of the Wharf and was traditionally where the dolphineers held conferences with pods or individuals. This was also where the dolphins came to report unusual occurrences to the Bay Watch or for rare instances when they required medical attention. The end timbers were smoother than the others due to the dolphins' habit of rubbing against them.

Above the float hung the Big Bell, its belfry sturdily attached to a massive six by six molded plastic pylon well-footed on the seafloor below. The chain the dolphins yanked to summon humans now idly

slapped against the pylon with the action of the light sea.

"We landfolk have trouble and need dolphin help," Jim said and pointed inland where the clouds of white and grey smoke curled ominously into the sky from two of the three previously extinct volcanoes. "We must leave this place and take from here all that can be moved. Do the other pods come?"

"Big trouble?" Teresa asked, leisurely swimming beyond the bulk of the Wharf to check the direction in which Jim had pointed. She raised herself high above the water, turning first one, then the other eye, to assess the situation. Her sides showed the rakings of many years' contact with amorous or angry males. "Big smoke. Worse than Young Mountain."

9

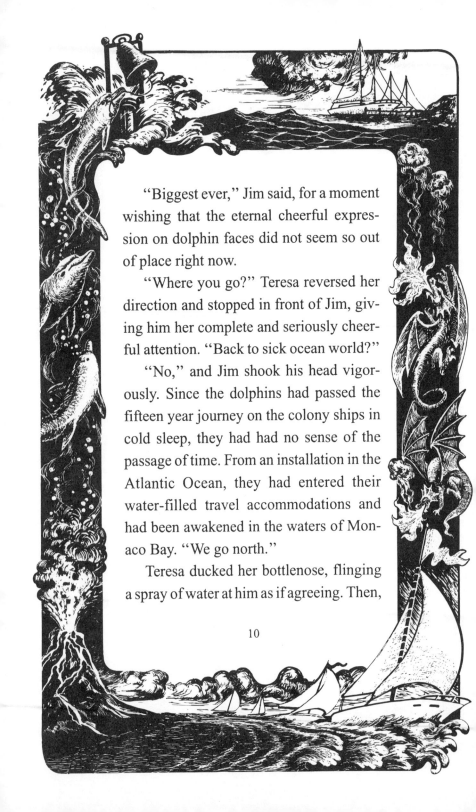

"Biggest ever," Jim said, for a moment wishing that the eternal cheerful expression on dolphin faces did not seem so out of place right now.

"Where you go?" Teresa reversed her direction and stopped in front of Jim, giving him her complete and seriously cheerful attention. "Back to sick ocean world?"

"No," and Jim shook his head vigorously. Since the dolphins had passed the fifteen year journey on the colony ships in cold sleep, they had had no sense of the passage of time. From an installation in the Atlantic Ocean, they had entered their water-filled travel accommodations and had been awakened in the waters of Monaco Bay. "We go north."

Teresa ducked her bottlenose, flinging a spray of water at him as if agreeing. Then,

10

dropping her head in the water, she gave forth to the members of her pod a rapid series of word noises too fast for Jim to follow though, over the past eight years on Pern, he'd learned a good deal of their vocabulary.

Kibby glided to one side of Teresa and Captiva bobbed up on the other, all earnestly regarding Jim.

"Sandman, Oregon," Captiva said distinctly, "are in West Flow. They turn, return as fast as the flux allows."

Then Aleta and Maxmillian abruptly arrived, adroitly avoiding a collision with the others. Pha pushed neatly in, too, as he was never one to be left out on the periphery.

"Echo from Cass. They speed back. New sun see them here," Pha said and blew

11

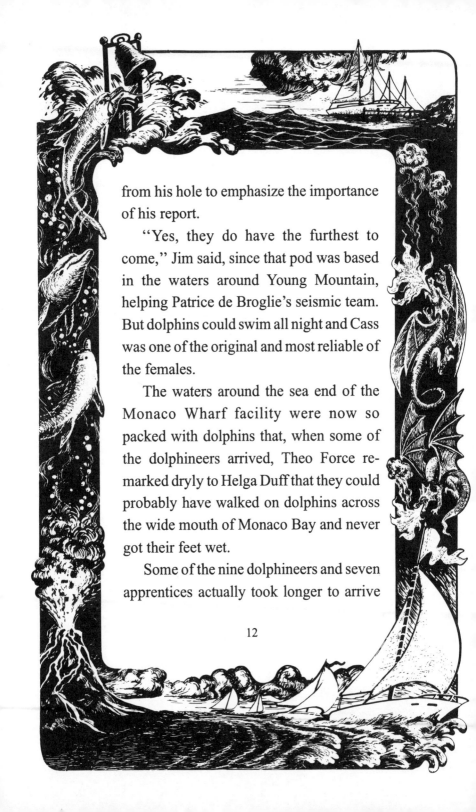

from his hole to emphasize the importance of his report.

"Yes, they do have the furthest to come," Jim said, since that pod was based in the waters around Young Mountain, helping Patrice de Broglie's seismic team. But dolphins could swim all night and Cass was one of the original and most reliable of the females.

The waters around the sea end of the Monaco Wharf facility were now so packed with dolphins that, when some of the dolphineers arrived, Theo Force remarked dryly to Helga Duff that they could probably have walked on dolphins across the wide mouth of Monaco Bay and never got their feet wet.

Some of the nine dolphineers and seven apprentices actually took longer to arrive

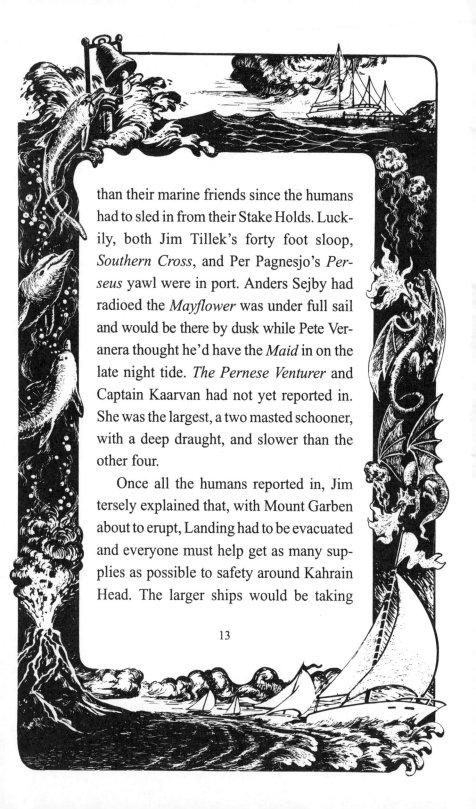

than their marine friends since the humans had to sled in from their Stake Holds. Luckily, both Jim Tillek's forty foot sloop, *Southern Cross*, and Per Pagnesjo's *Perseus* yawl were in port. Anders Sejby had radioed the *Mayflower* was under full sail and would be there by dusk while Pete Veranera thought he'd have the *Maid* in on the late night tide. *The Pernese Venturer* and Captain Kaarvan had not yet reported in. She was the largest, a two masted schooner, with a deep draught, and slower than the other four.

Once all the humans reported in, Jim tersely explained that, with Mount Garben about to erupt, Landing had to be evacuated and everyone must help get as many supplies as possible to safety around Kahrain Head. The larger ships would be taking

13

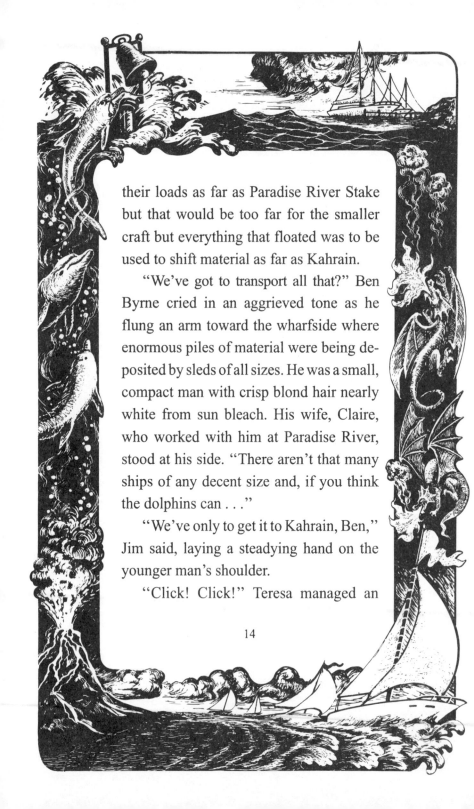

their loads as far as Paradise River Stake but that would be too far for the smaller craft but everything that floated was to be used to shift material as far as Kahrain.

"We've got to transport all that?" Ben Byrne cried in an aggrieved tone as he flung an arm toward the wharfside where enormous piles of material were being deposited by sleds of all sizes. He was a small, compact man with crisp blond hair nearly white from sun bleach. His wife, Claire, who worked with him at Paradise River, stood at his side. "There aren't that many ships of any decent size and, if you think the dolphins can . . ."

"We've only to get it to Kahrain, Ben," Jim said, laying a steadying hand on the younger man's shoulder.

"Click! Click!" Teresa managed an

14

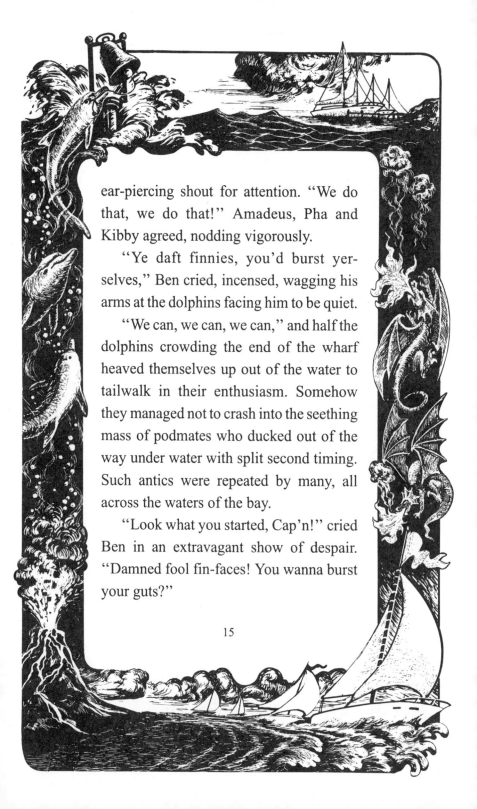

ear-piercing shout for attention. "We do that, we do that!" Amadeus, Pha and Kibby agreed, nodding vigorously.

"Ye daft finnies, you'd burst yer-selves," Ben cried, incensed, wagging his arms at the dolphins facing him to be quiet.

"We can, we can, we can," and half the dolphins crowding the end of the wharf heaved themselves up out of the water to tailwalk in their enthusiasm. Somehow they managed not to crash into the seething mass of podmates who ducked out of the way under water with split second timing. Such antics were repeated by many, all across the waters of the bay.

"Look what you started, Cap'n!" cried Ben in an extravagant show of despair. "Damned fool fin-faces! You wanna burst your guts?"

15

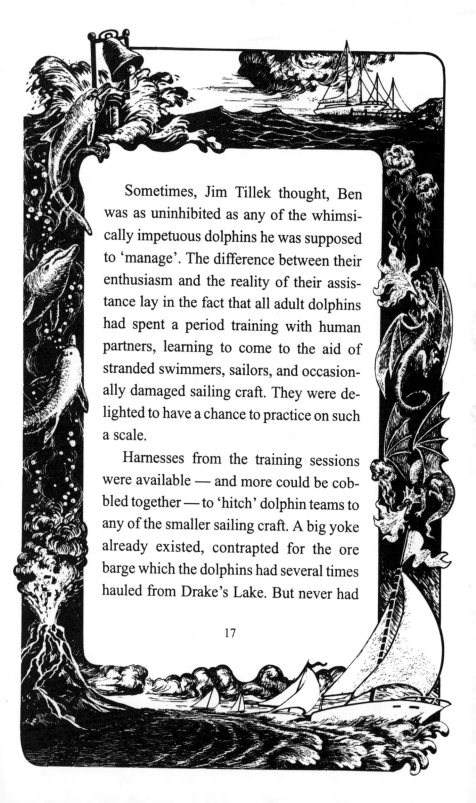

Sometimes, Jim Tillek thought, Ben was as uninhibited as any of the whimsically impetuous dolphins he was supposed to 'manage'. The difference between their enthusiasm and the reality of their assistance lay in the fact that all adult dolphins had spent a period training with human partners, learning to come to the aid of stranded swimmers, sailors, and occasionally damaged sailing craft. They were delighted to have a chance to practice on such a scale.

Harnesses from the training sessions were available — and more could be cobbled together — to 'hitch' dolphin teams to any of the smaller sailing craft. A big yoke already existed, contrapted for the ore barge which the dolphins had several times hauled from Drake's Lake. But never had

17

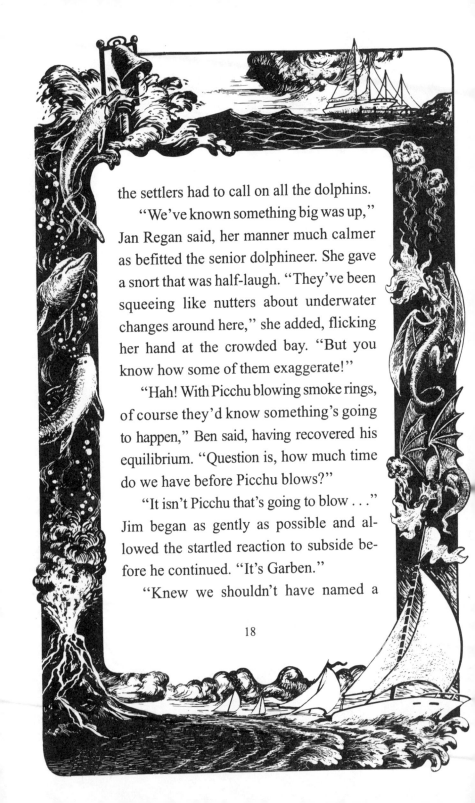

the settlers had to call on all the dolphins.

"We've known something big was up," Jan Regan said, her manner much calmer as befitted the senior dolphineer. She gave a snort that was half-laugh. "They've been squeeing like nutters about underwater changes around here," she added, flicking her hand at the crowded bay. "But you know how some of them exaggerate!"

"Hah! With Picchu blowing smoke rings, of course they'd know something's going to happen," Ben said, having recovered his equilibrium. "Question is, how much time do we have before Picchu blows?"

"It isn't Picchu that's going to blow . . ." Jim began as gently as possible and allowed the startled reaction to subside before he continued. "It's Garben."

"Knew we shouldn't have named a

18

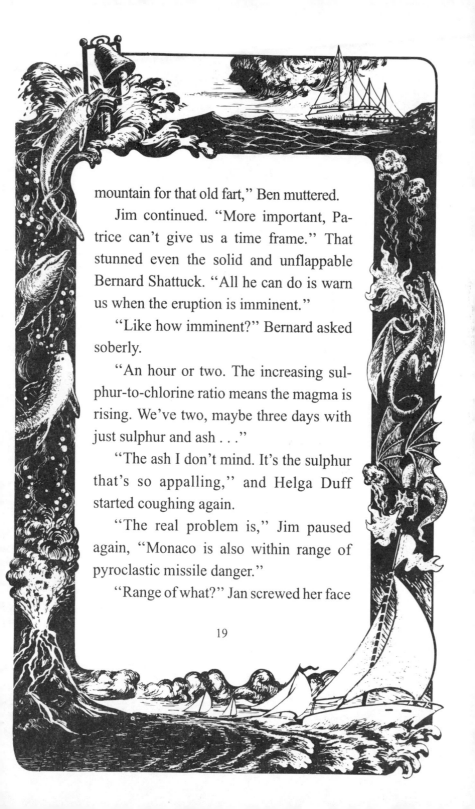

mountain for that old fart," Ben muttered.

Jim continued. "More important, Patrice can't give us a time frame." That stunned even the solid and unflappable Bernard Shattuck. "All he can do is warn us when the eruption is imminent."

"Like how imminent?" Bernard asked soberly.

"An hour or two. The increasing sulphur-to-chlorine ratio means the magma is rising. We've two, maybe three days with just sulphur and ash . . ."

"The ash I don't mind. It's the sulphur that's so appalling," and Helga Duff started coughing again.

"The real problem is," Jim paused again, "Monaco is also within range of pyroclastic missile danger."

"Range of what?" Jan screwed her face

19

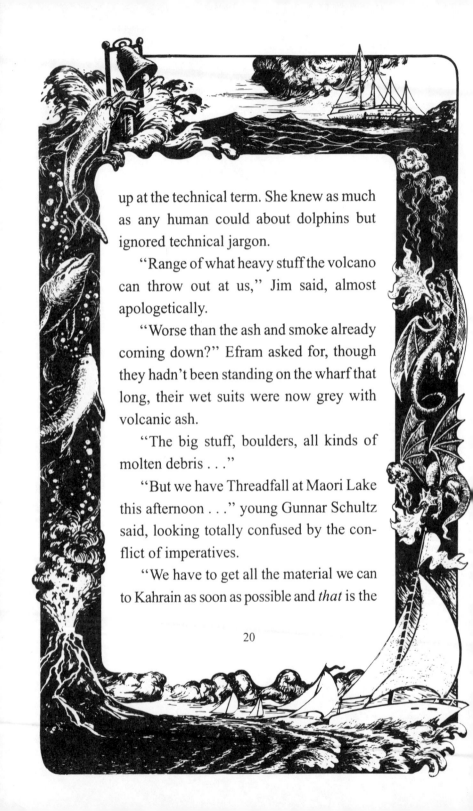

up at the technical term. She knew as much as any human could about dolphins but ignored technical jargon.

"Range of what heavy stuff the volcano can throw out at us," Jim said, almost apologetically.

"Worse than the ash and smoke already coming down?" Efram asked for, though they hadn't been standing on the wharf that long, their wet suits were now grey with volcanic ash.

"The big stuff, boulders, all kinds of molten debris . . ."

"But we have Threadfall at Maori Lake this afternoon . . ." young Gunnar Schultz said, looking totally confused by the conflict of imperatives.

"We have to get all the material we can to Kahrain as soon as possible and *that* is the

20

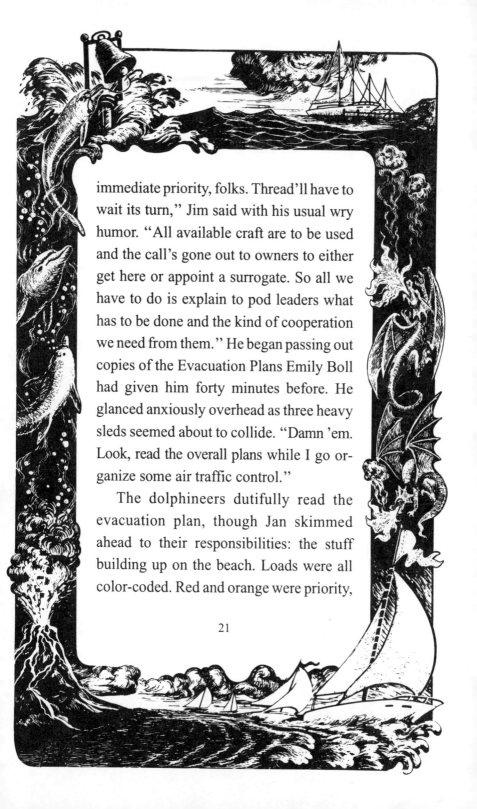

immediate priority, folks. Thread'll have to wait its turn," Jim said with his usual wry humor. "All available craft are to be used and the call's gone out to owners to either get here or appoint a surrogate. So all we have to do is explain to pod leaders what has to be done and the kind of cooperation we need from them." He began passing out copies of the Evacuation Plans Emily Boll had given him forty minutes before. He glanced anxiously overhead as three heavy sleds seemed about to collide. "Damn 'em. Look, read the overall plans while I go organize some air traffic control."

The dolphineers dutifully read the evacuation plan, though Jan skimmed ahead to their responsibilities: the stuff building up on the beach. Loads were all color-coded. Red and orange were priority,

21

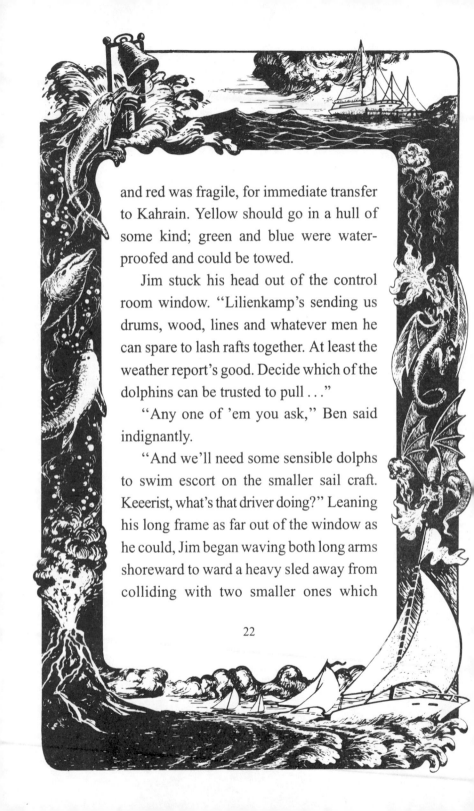

and red was fragile, for immediate transfer to Kahrain. Yellow should go in a hull of some kind; green and blue were water-proofed and could be towed.

Jim stuck his head out of the control room window. "Lilienkamp's sending us drums, wood, lines and whatever men he can spare to lash rafts together. At least the weather report's good. Decide which of the dolphins can be trusted to pull ..."

"Any one of 'em you ask," Ben said indignantly.

"And we'll need some sensible dolphs to swim escort on the smaller sail craft. Keeerist, what's that driver doing?" Leaning his long frame as far out of the window as he could, Jim began waving both long arms shoreward to ward a heavy sled away from colliding with two smaller ones which

22

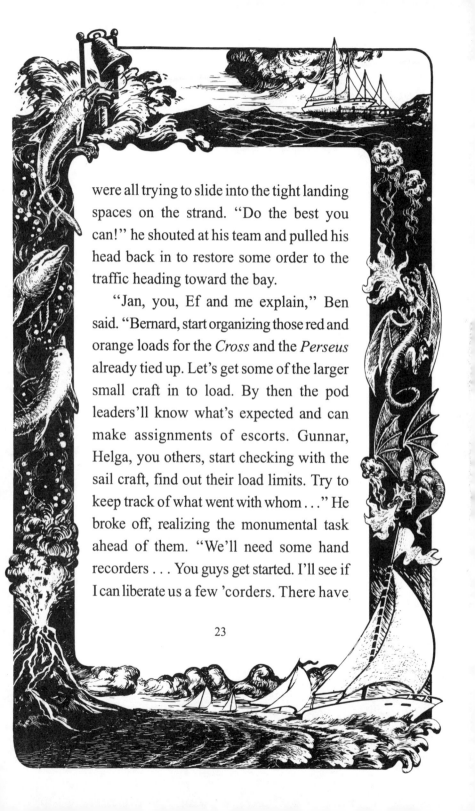

were all trying to slide into the tight landing spaces on the strand. "Do the best you can!" he shouted at his team and pulled his head back in to restore some order to the traffic heading toward the bay.

"Jan, you, Ef and me explain," Ben said. "Bernard, start organizing those red and orange loads for the *Cross* and the *Perseus* already tied up. Let's get some of the larger small craft in to load. By then the pod leaders'll know what's expected and can make assignments of escorts. Gunnar, Helga, you others, start checking with the sail craft, find out their load limits. Try to keep track of what went with whom . . ." He broke off, realizing the monumental task ahead of them. "We'll need some hand recorders . . . You guys get started. I'll see if I can liberate us a few 'corders. There have

23

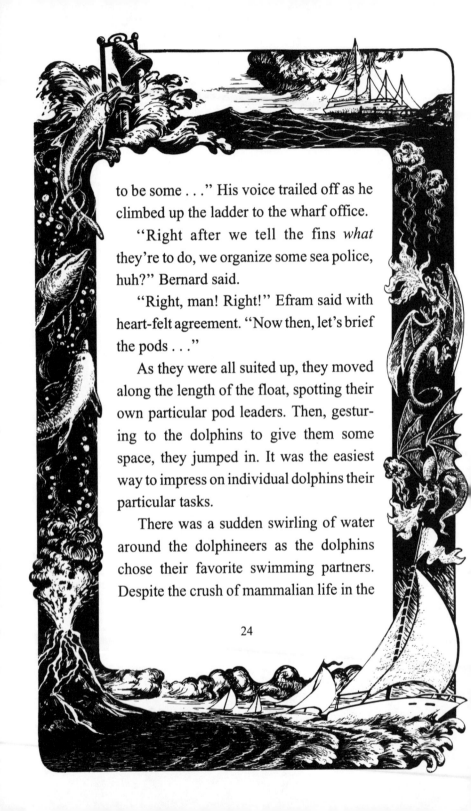

to be some . . ." His voice trailed off as he climbed up the ladder to the wharf office.

"Right after we tell the fins *what* they're to do, we organize some sea police, huh?" Bernard said.

"Right, man! Right!" Efram said with heart-felt agreement. "Now then, let's brief the pods . . ."

As they were all suited up, they moved along the length of the float, spotting their own particular pod leaders. Then, gesturing to the dolphins to give them some space, they jumped in. It was the easiest way to impress on individual dolphins their particular tasks.

There was a sudden swirling of water around the dolphineers as the dolphins chose their favorite swimming partners. Despite the crush of mammalian life in the

24

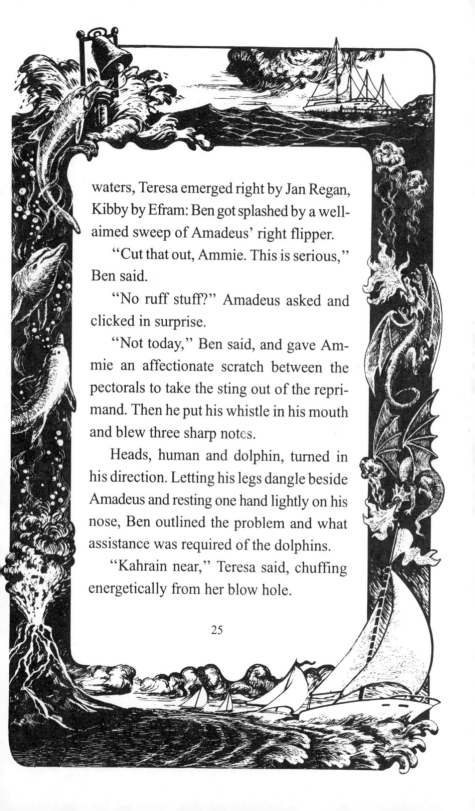

waters, Teresa emerged right by Jan Regan, Kibby by Efram: Ben got splashed by a well-aimed sweep of Amadeus' right flipper.

"Cut that out, Ammie. This is serious," Ben said.

"No ruff stuff?" Amadeus asked and clicked in surprise.

"Not today," Ben said, and gave Ammie an affectionate scratch between the pectorals to take the sting out of the reprimand. Then he put his whistle in his mouth and blew three sharp notes.

Heads, human and dolphin, turned in his direction. Letting his legs dangle beside Amadeus and resting one hand lightly on his nose, Ben outlined the problem and what assistance was required of the dolphins.

"Kahrain near," Teresa said, chuffing energetically from her blow hole.

25

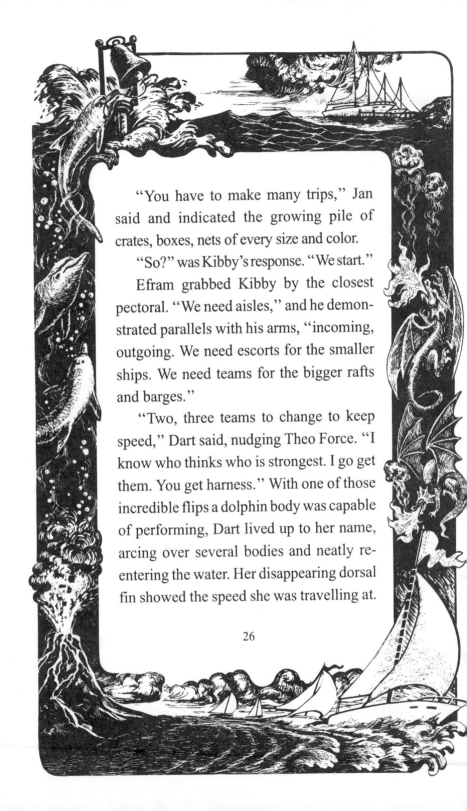

"You have to make many trips," Jan said and indicated the growing pile of crates, boxes, nets of every size and color.

"So?" was Kibby's response. "We start."

Efram grabbed Kibby by the closest pectoral. "We need aisles," and he demonstrated parallels with his arms, "incoming, outgoing. We need escorts for the smaller ships. We need teams for the bigger rafts and barges."

"Two, three teams to change to keep speed," Dart said, nudging Theo Force. "I know who thinks who is strongest. I go get them. You get harness." With one of those incredible flips a dolphin body was capable of performing, Dart lived up to her name, arcing over several bodies and neatly reentering the water. Her disappearing dorsal fin showed the speed she was travelling at.

26

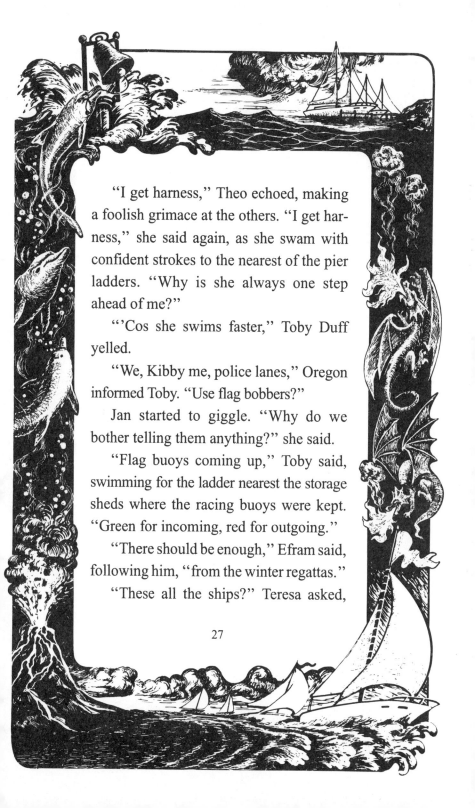

"I get harness," Theo echoed, making a foolish grimace at the others. "I get harness," she said again, as she swam with confident strokes to the nearest of the pier ladders. "Why is she always one step ahead of me?"

"'Cos she swims faster," Toby Duff yelled.

"We, Kibby me, police lanes," Oregon informed Toby. "Use flag bobbers?"

Jan started to giggle. "Why do we bother telling them anything?" she said.

"Flag buoys coming up," Toby said, swimming for the ladder nearest the storage sheds where the racing buoys were kept. "Green for incoming, red for outgoing."

"There should be enough," Efram said, following him, "from the winter regattas."

"These all the ships?" Teresa asked,

27

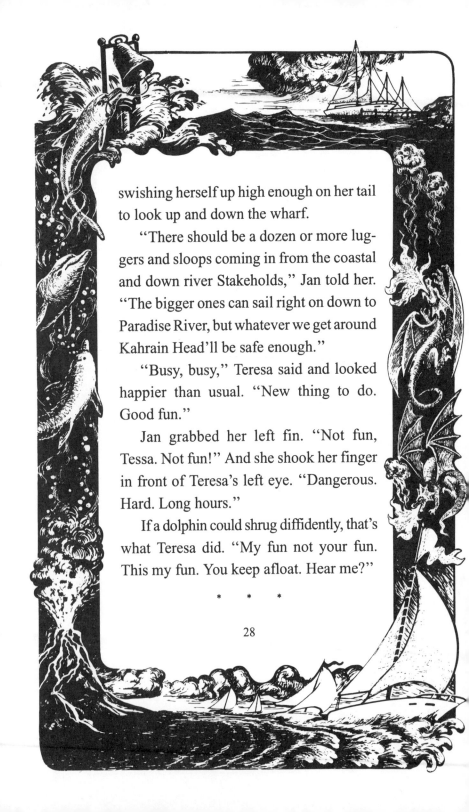

swishing herself up high enough on her tail to look up and down the wharf.

"There should be a dozen or more luggers and sloops coming in from the coastal and down river Stakeholds," Jan told her. "The bigger ones can sail right on down to Paradise River, but whatever we get around Kahrain Head'll be safe enough."

"Busy, busy," Teresa said and looked happier than usual. "New thing to do. Good fun."

Jan grabbed her left fin. "Not fun, Tessa. Not fun!" And she shook her finger in front of Teresa's left eye. "Dangerous. Hard. Long hours."

If a dolphin could shrug diffidently, that's what Teresa did. "My fun not your fun. This my fun. You keep afloat. Hear me?"

\* \* \*

28

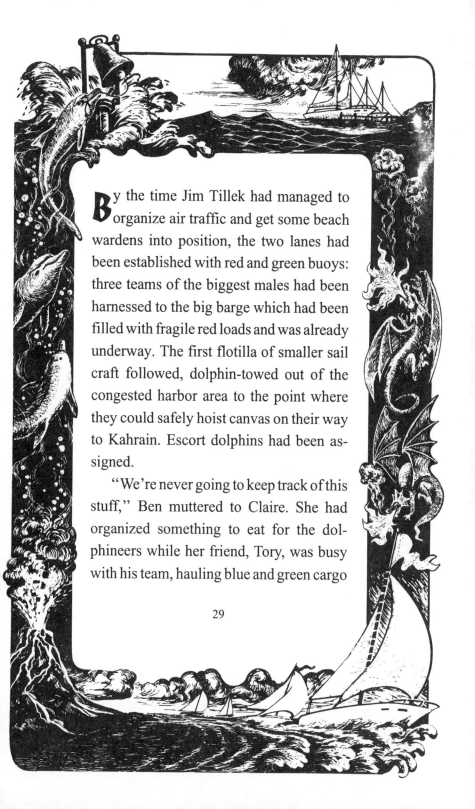

By the time Jim Tillek had managed to organize air traffic and get some beach wardens into position, the two lanes had been established with red and green buoys: three teams of the biggest males had been harnessed to the big barge which had been filled with fragile red loads and was already underway. The first flotilla of smaller sail craft followed, dolphin-towed out of the congested harbor area to the point where they could safely hoist canvas on their way to Kahrain. Escort dolphins had been assigned.

"We're never going to keep track of this stuff," Ben muttered to Claire. She had organized something to eat for the dolphineers while her friend, Tory, was busy with his team, hauling blue and green cargo

29

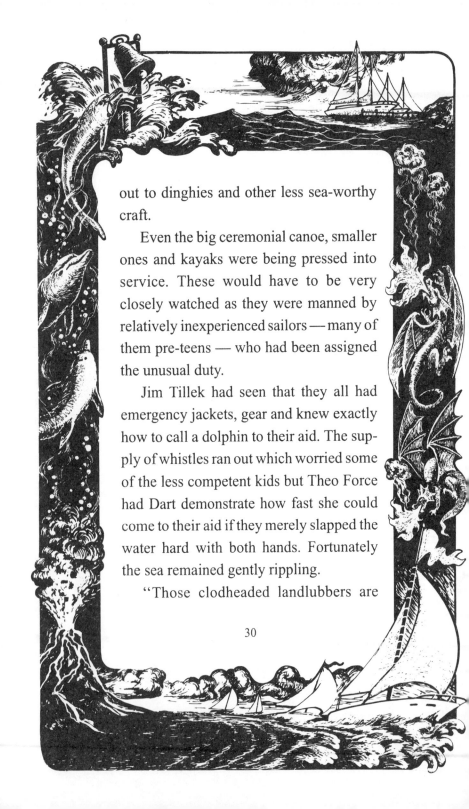

out to dinghies and other less sea-worthy craft.

Even the big ceremonial canoe, smaller ones and kayaks were being pressed into service. These would have to be very closely watched as they were manned by relatively inexperienced sailors — many of them pre-teens — who had been assigned the unusual duty.

Jim Tillek had seen that they all had emergency jackets, gear and knew exactly how to call a dolphin to their aid. The supply of whistles ran out which worried some of the less competent kids but Theo Force had Dart demonstrate how fast she could come to their aid if they merely slapped the water hard with both hands. Fortunately the sea remained gently rippling.

"Those clodheaded landlubbers are

30

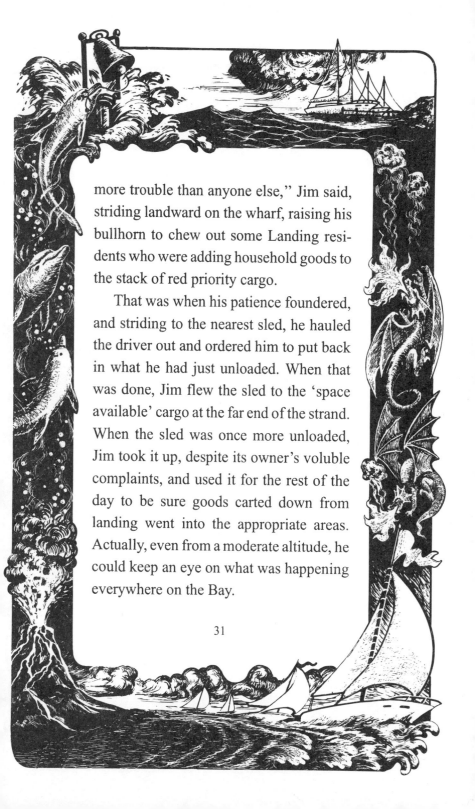

more trouble than anyone else," Jim said, striding landward on the wharf, raising his bullhorn to chew out some Landing residents who were adding household goods to the stack of red priority cargo.

That was when his patience foundered, and striding to the nearest sled, he hauled the driver out and ordered him to put back in what he had just unloaded. When that was done, Jim flew the sled to the 'space available' cargo at the far end of the strand. When the sled was once more unloaded, Jim took it up, despite its owner's voluble complaints, and used it for the rest of the day to be sure goods carted down from landing went into the appropriate areas. Actually, even from a moderate altitude, he could keep an eye on what was happening everywhere on the Bay.

31

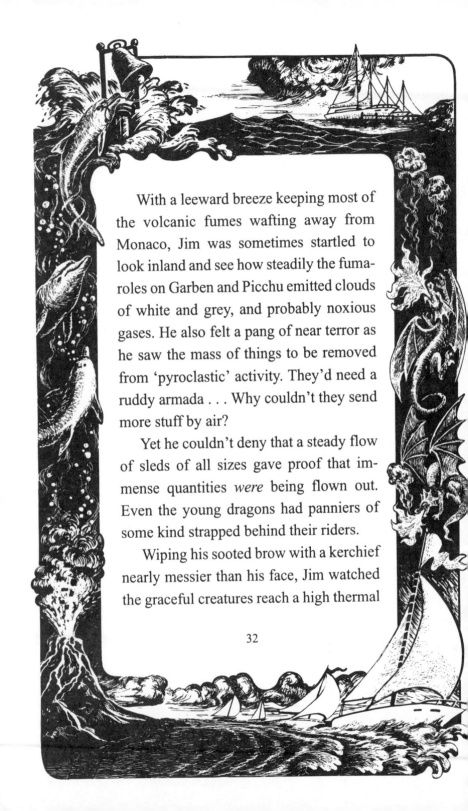

With a leeward breeze keeping most of
the volcanic fumes wafting away from
Monaco, Jim was sometimes startled to
look inland and see how steadily the fuma-
roles on Garben and Picchu emitted clouds
of white and grey, and probably noxious
gases. He also felt a pang of near terror as
he saw the mass of things to be removed
from 'pyroclastic' activity. They'd need a
ruddy armada . . . Why couldn't they send
more stuff by air?

Yet he couldn't deny that a steady flow
of sleds of all sizes gave proof that im-
mense quantities *were* being flown out.
Even the young dragons had panniers of
some kind strapped behind their riders.

Wiping his sooted brow with a kerchief
nearly messier than his face, Jim watched
the graceful creatures reach a high thermal

32

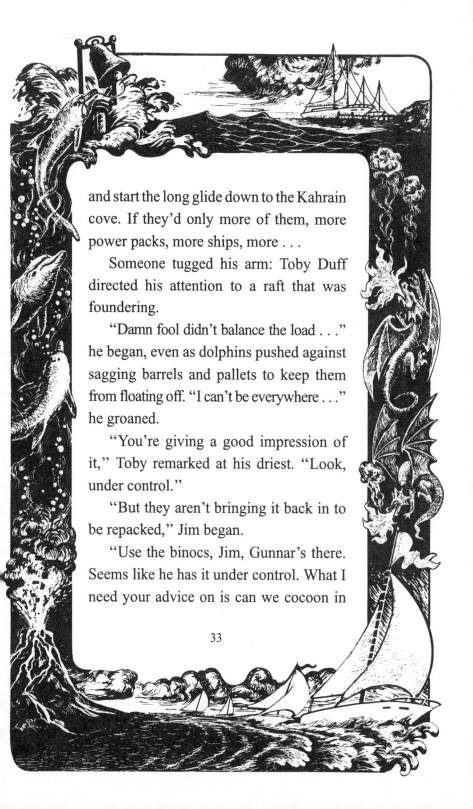

and start the long glide down to the Kahrain cove. If they'd only more of them, more power packs, more ships, more . . .

Someone tugged his arm: Toby Duff directed his attention to a raft that was foundering.

"Damn fool didn't balance the load . . ." he began, even as dolphins pushed against sagging barrels and pallets to keep them from floating off. "I can't be everywhere . . ." he groaned.

"You're giving a good impression of it," Toby remarked at his driest. "Look, under control."

"But they aren't bringing it back in to be repacked," Jim began.

"Use the binocs, Jim, Gunnar's there. Seems like he has it under control. What I need your advice on is can we cocoon in

33

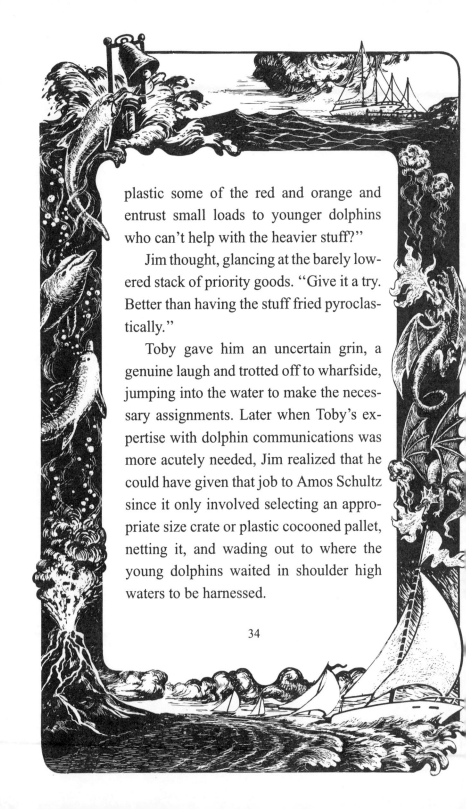

plastic some of the red and orange and entrust small loads to younger dolphins who can't help with the heavier stuff?"

Jim thought, glancing at the barely lowered stack of priority goods. "Give it a try. Better than having the stuff fried pyroclastically."

Toby gave him an uncertain grin, a genuine laugh and trotted off to wharfside, jumping into the water to make the necessary assignments. Later when Toby's expertise with dolphin communications was more acutely needed, Jim realized that he could have given that job to Amos Schultz since it only involved selecting an appropriate size crate or plastic cocooned pallet, netting it, and wading out to where the young dolphins waited in shoulder high waters to be harnessed.

34

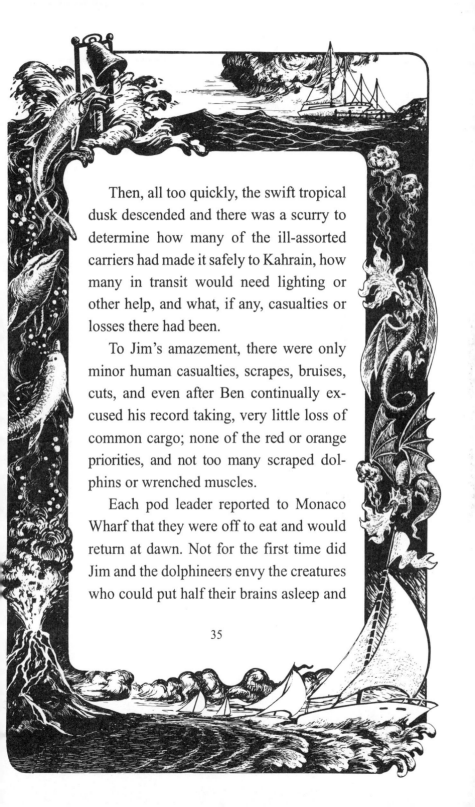

Then, all too quickly, the swift tropical dusk descended and there was a scurry to determine how many of the ill-assorted carriers had made it safely to Kahrain, how many in transit would need lighting or other help, and what, if any, casualties or losses there had been.

To Jim's amazement, there were only minor human casualties, scrapes, bruises, cuts, and even after Ben continually excused his record taking, very little loss of common cargo; none of the red or orange priorities, and not too many scraped dolphins or wrenched muscles.

Each pod leader reported to Monaco Wharf that they were off to eat and would return at dawn. Not for the first time did Jim and the dolphineers envy the creatures who could put half their brains asleep and

35

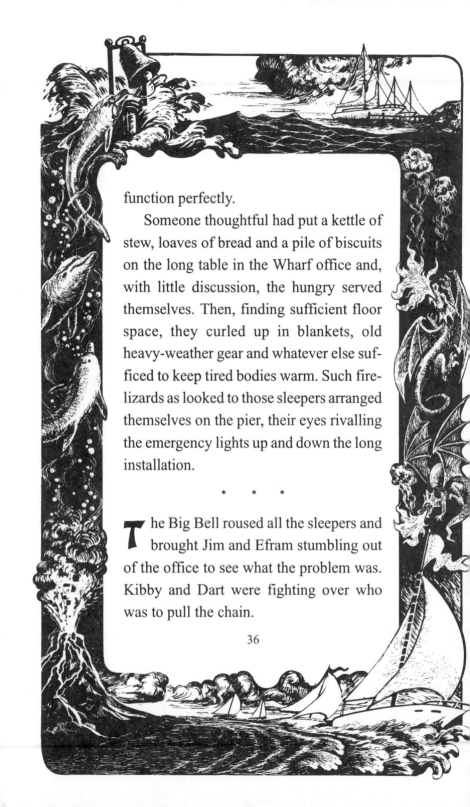

function perfectly.

Someone thoughtful had put a kettle of stew, loaves of bread and a pile of biscuits on the long table in the Wharf office and, with little discussion, the hungry served themselves. Then, finding sufficient floor space, they curled up in blankets, old heavy-weather gear and whatever else sufficed to keep tired bodies warm. Such fire-lizards as looked to those sleepers arranged themselves on the pier, their eyes rivalling the emergency lights up and down the long installation.

\*　　\*　　\*

The Big Bell roused all the sleepers and brought Jim and Efram stumbling out of the office to see what the problem was. Kibby and Dart were fighting over who was to pull the chain.

36

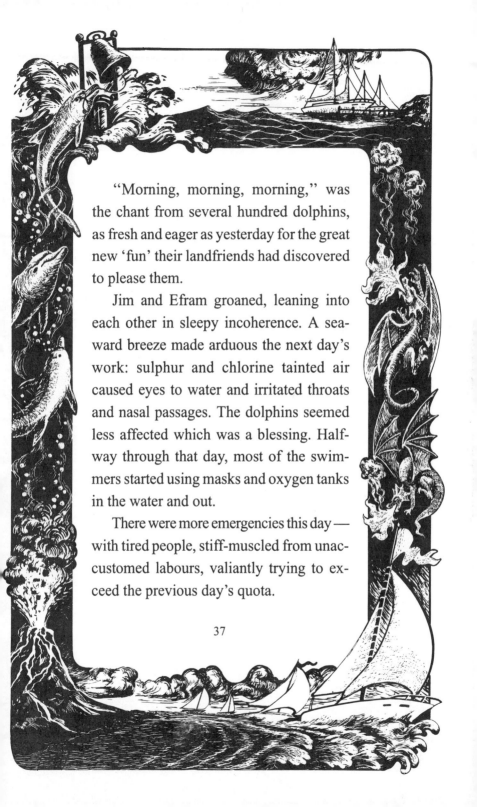

"Morning, morning, morning," was the chant from several hundred dolphins, as fresh and eager as yesterday for the great new 'fun' their landfriends had discovered to please them.

Jim and Efram groaned, leaning into each other in sleepy incoherence. A seaward breeze made arduous the next day's work: sulphur and chlorine tainted air caused eyes to water and irritated throats and nasal passages. The dolphins seemed less affected which was a blessing. Halfway through that day, most of the swimmers started using masks and oxygen tanks in the water and out.

There were more emergencies this day — with tired people, stiff-muscled from unaccustomed labours, valiantly trying to exceed the previous day's quota.

37

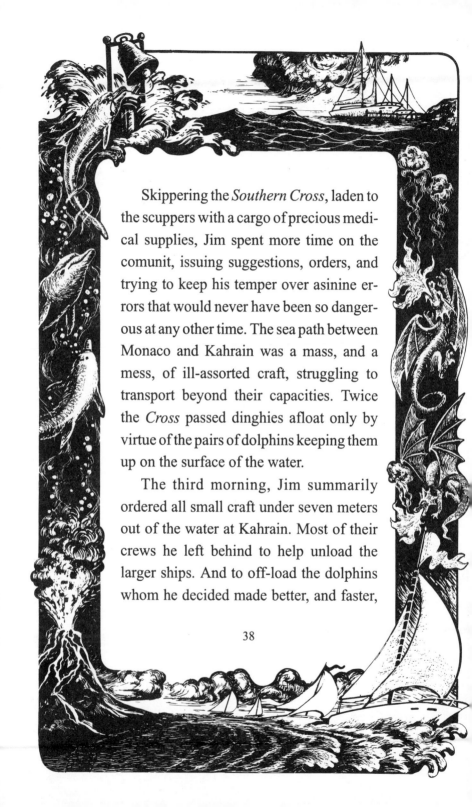

Skippering the *Southern Cross*, laden to the scuppers with a cargo of precious medical supplies, Jim spent more time on the comunit, issuing suggestions, orders, and trying to keep his temper over asinine errors that would never have been so dangerous at any other time. The sea path between Monaco and Kahrain was a mass, and a mess, of ill-assorted craft, struggling to transport beyond their capacities. Twice the *Cross* passed dinghies afloat only by virtue of the pairs of dolphins keeping them up on the surface of the water.

The third morning, Jim summarily ordered all small craft under seven meters out of the water at Kahrain. Most of their crews he left behind to help unload the larger ships. And to off-load the dolphins whom he decided made better, and faster,

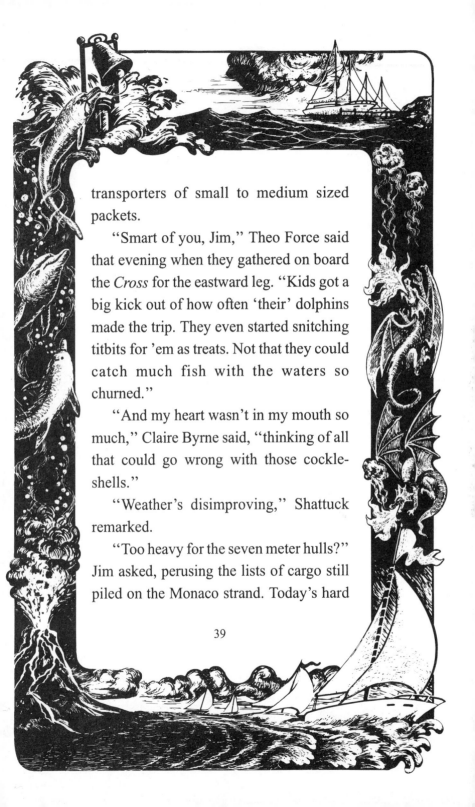

transporters of small to medium sized packets.

"Smart of you, Jim," Theo Force said that evening when they gathered on board the *Cross* for the eastward leg. "Kids got a big kick out of how often 'their' dolphins made the trip. They even started snitching titbits for 'em as treats. Not that they could catch much fish with the waters so churned."

"And my heart wasn't in my mouth so much," Claire Byrne said, "thinking of all that could go wrong with those cockle-shells."

"Weather's disimproving," Shattuck remarked.

"Too heavy for the seven meter hulls?" Jim asked, perusing the lists of cargo still piled on the Monaco strand. Today's hard

39

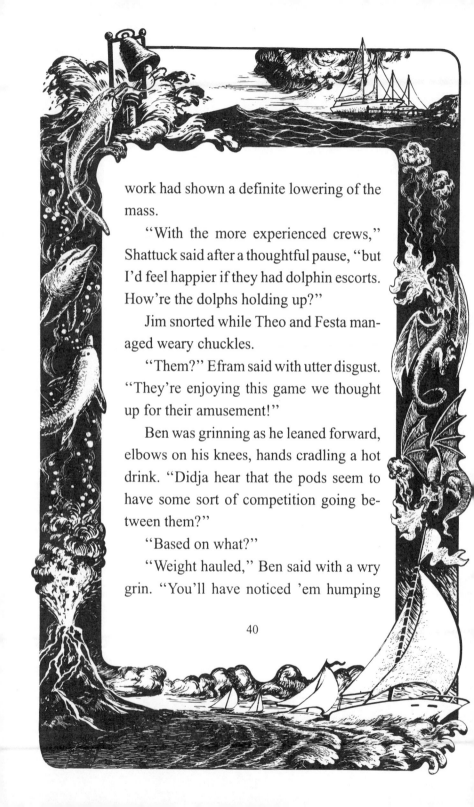

work had shown a definite lowering of the mass.

"With the more experienced crews," Shattuck said after a thoughtful pause, "but I'd feel happier if they had dolphin escorts. How're the dolphs holding up?"

Jim snorted while Theo and Festa managed weary chuckles.

"Them?" Efram said with utter disgust. "They're enjoying this game we thought up for their amusement!"

Ben was grinning as he leaned forward, elbows on his knees, hands cradling a hot drink. "Didja hear that the pods seem to have some sort of competition going between them?"

"Based on what?"

"Weight hauled," Ben said with a wry grin. "You'll have noticed 'em humping

40

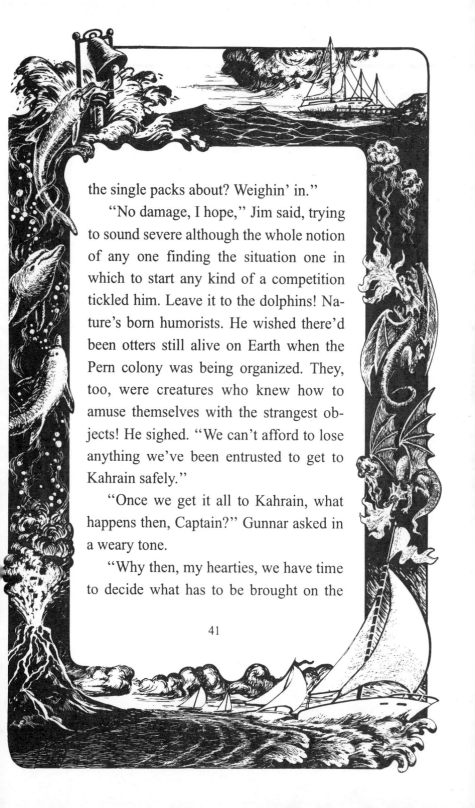

the single packs about? Weighin' in."

"No damage, I hope," Jim said, trying to sound severe although the whole notion of any one finding the situation one in which to start any kind of a competition tickled him. Leave it to the dolphins! Nature's born humorists. He wished there'd been otters still alive on Earth when the Pern colony was being organized. They, too, were creatures who knew how to amuse themselves with the strangest objects! He sighed. "We can't afford to lose anything we've been entrusted to get to Kahrain safely."

"Once we get it all to Kahrain, what happens then, Captain?" Gunnar asked in a weary tone.

"Why then, my hearties, we have time to decide what has to be brought on the

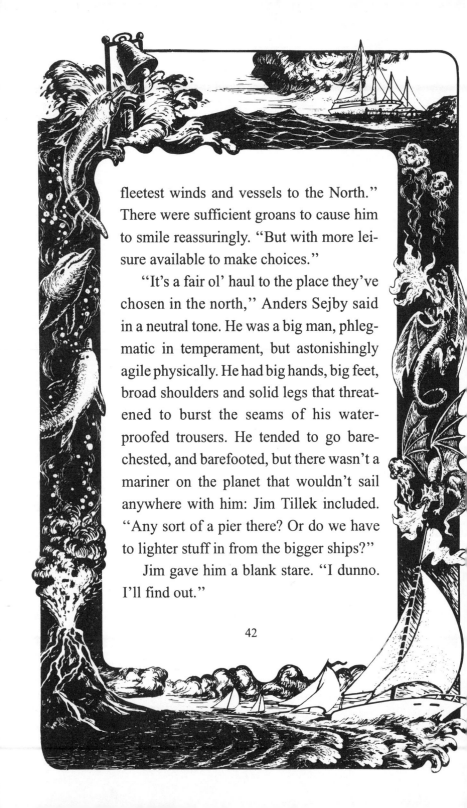

fleetest winds and vessels to the North."
There were sufficient groans to cause him
to smile reassuringly. "But with more lei-
sure available to make choices."

"It's a fair ol' haul to the place they've
chosen in the north," Anders Sejby said
in a neutral tone. He was a big man, phleg-
matic in temperament, but astonishingly
agile physically. He had big hands, big feet,
broad shoulders and solid legs that threat-
ened to burst the seams of his water-
proofed trousers. He tended to go bare-
chested, and barefooted, but there wasn't a
mariner on the planet that wouldn't sail
anywhere with him: Jim Tillek included.
"Any sort of a pier there? Or do we have
to lighter stuff in from the bigger ships?"

Jim gave him a blank stare. "I dunno.
I'll find out."

"You mean," asked Ben who fired up easily, "we're busting our nuts doing all this and we've got to . . ."

Speaking into his comunit, Jim held up his hand to stem Ben's indignant protest. "All will be prepared for us there."

"Bet it wasn't until you mentioned it," Ben said sourly.

"Be not of faint heart, Ben," Jim said, laying his hand in a benedictory fashion on the dolphineer's salt encrusted curls. "By the time we get there, we'll have wharf facilities. Paul Benden solemnly promised me." Ben snorted, unrepentant. "Now, let's sort out what we've got to move tomorrow."

Garben moved first. The warning Patrice sent out gave them a scant two hours and the advice that everything that could

43

leave Monaco should be gone well before that time limit. No one had any coherent memories of that period. Neither of the bigger ships, the *Cross* or the *Perseus,* were fully loaded when the alarm came. They were sailed far enough out of the projected danger area. If the wharf, and the cargo, was left when the eruption was over, they would go back in and finish loading.

Everyone did have memories of Garben's spectacular eruption, seen at a safe enough distance to be clear of the 'pyroclastic' debris. It was truly awe-inspiring, and immensely heartbreaking, to see the community that they had achieved in such a short time showered with ash, burning missiles, and disappearing behind dense grey clouds.

"Did everyone get out?" Theo called

44

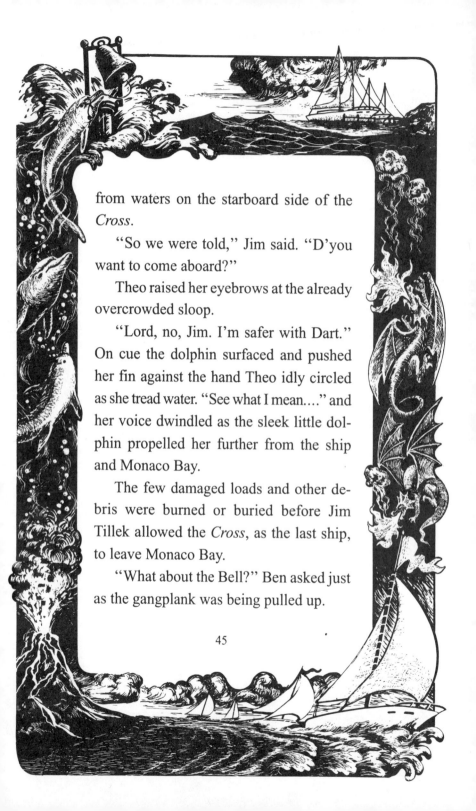

from waters on the starboard side of the *Cross*.

"So we were told," Jim said. "D'you want to come aboard?"

Theo raised her eyebrows at the already overcrowded sloop.

"Lord, no, Jim. I'm safer with Dart." On cue the dolphin surfaced and pushed her fin against the hand Theo idly circled as she tread water. "See what I mean...." and her voice dwindled as the sleek little dolphin propelled her further from the ship and Monaco Bay.

The few damaged loads and other debris were burned or buried before Jim Tillek allowed the *Cross*, as the last ship, to leave Monaco Bay.

"What about the Bell?" Ben asked just as the gangplank was being pulled up.

45

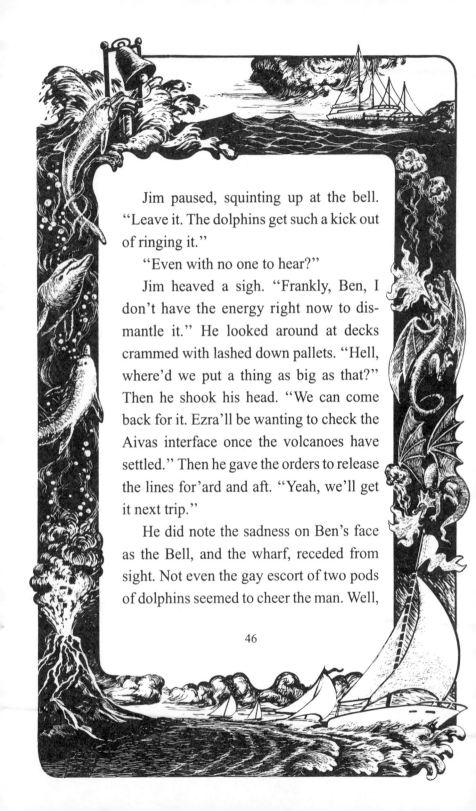

Jim paused, squinting up at the bell. "Leave it. The dolphins get such a kick out of ringing it."

"Even with no one to hear?"

Jim heaved a sigh. "Frankly, Ben, I don't have the energy right now to dismantle it." He looked around at decks crammed with lashed down pallets. "Hell, where'd we put a thing as big as that?" Then he shook his head. "We can come back for it. Ezra'll be wanting to check the Aivas interface once the volcanoes have settled." Then he gave the orders to release the lines for'ard and aft. "Yeah, we'll get it next trip."

He did note the sadness on Ben's face as the Bell, and the wharf, receded from sight. Not even the gay escort of two pods of dolphins seemed to cheer the man. Well,

46

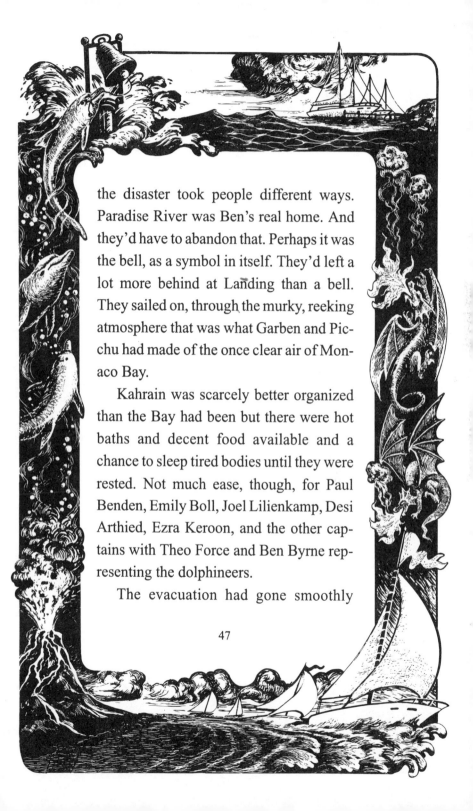

the disaster took people different ways. Paradise River was Ben's real home. And they'd have to abandon that. Perhaps it was the bell, as a symbol in itself. They'd left a lot more behind at Landing than a bell. They sailed on, through the murky, reeking atmosphere that was what Garben and Picchu had made of the once clear air of Monaco Bay.

Kahrain was scarcely better organized than the Bay had been but there were hot baths and decent food available and a chance to sleep tired bodies until they were rested. Not much ease, though, for Paul Benden, Emily Boll, Joel Lilienkamp, Desi Arthied, Ezra Keroon, and the other captains with Theo Force and Ben Byrne representing the dolphineers.

The evacuation had gone smoothly

47

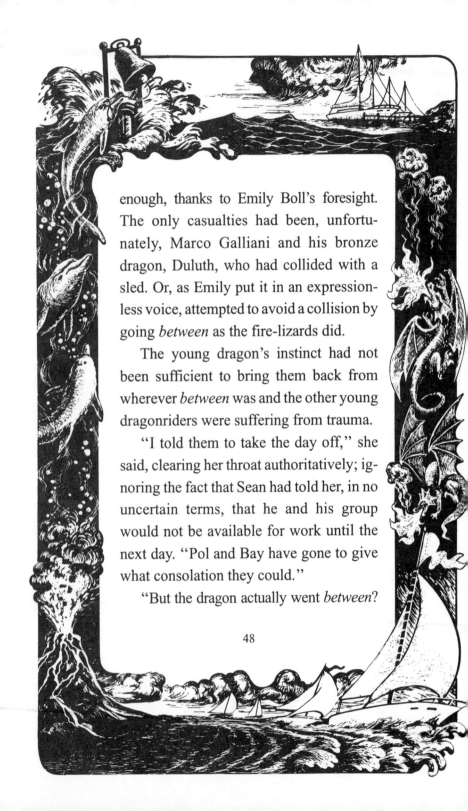

enough, thanks to Emily Boll's foresight. The only casualties had been, unfortunately, Marco Galliani and his bronze dragon, Duluth, who had collided with a sled. Or, as Emily put it in an expressionless voice, attempted to avoid a collision by going *between* as the fire-lizards did.

The young dragon's instinct had not been sufficient to bring them back from wherever *between* was and the other young dragonriders were suffering from trauma.

"I told them to take the day off," she said, clearing her throat authoritatively; ignoring the fact that Sean had told her, in no uncertain terms, that he and his group would not be available for work until the next day. "Pol and Bay have gone to give what consolation they could."

"But the dragon actually went *between*?

48

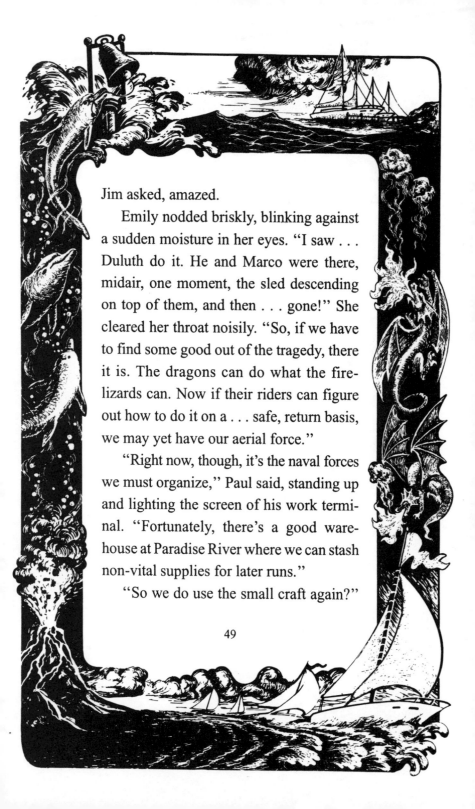

Jim asked, amazed.

Emily nodded briskly, blinking against a sudden moisture in her eyes. "I saw . . . Duluth do it. He and Marco were there, midair, one moment, the sled descending on top of them, and then . . . gone!" She cleared her throat noisily. "So, if we have to find some good out of the tragedy, there it is. The dragons can do what the fire-lizards can. Now if their riders can figure out how to do it on a . . . safe, return basis, we may yet have our aerial force."

"Right now, though, it's the naval forces we must organize," Paul said, standing up and lighting the screen of his work terminal. "Fortunately, there's a good warehouse at Paradise River where we can stash non-vital supplies for later runs."

"So we do use the small craft again?"

49

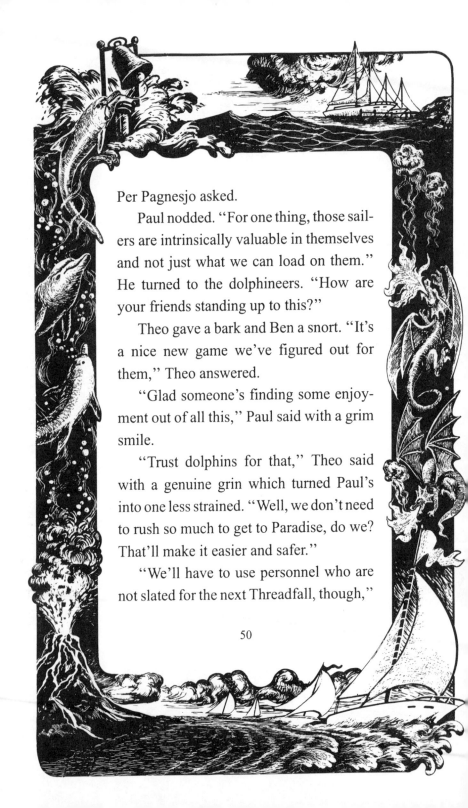

Per Pagnesjo asked.

Paul nodded. "For one thing, those sailers are intrinsically valuable in themselves and not just what we can load on them." He turned to the dolphineers. "How are your friends standing up to this?"

Theo gave a bark and Ben a snort. "It's a nice new game we've figured out for them," Theo answered.

"Glad someone's finding some enjoyment out of all this," Paul said with a grim smile.

"Trust dolphins for that," Theo said with a genuine grin which turned Paul's into one less strained. "Well, we don't need to rush so much to get to Paradise, do we? That'll make it easier and safer."

"We'll have to use personnel who are not slated for the next Threadfall, though,"

50

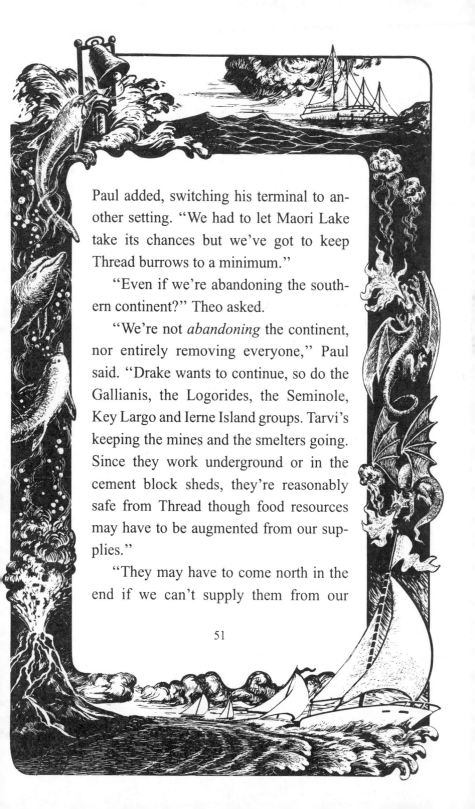

Paul added, switching his terminal to another setting. "We had to let Maori Lake take its chances but we've got to keep Thread burrows to a minimum."

"Even if we're abandoning the southern continent?" Theo asked.

"We're not *abandoning* the continent, nor entirely removing everyone," Paul said. "Drake wants to continue, so do the Gallianis, the Logorides, the Seminole, Key Largo and Ierne Island groups. Tarvi's keeping the mines and the smelters going. Since they work underground or in the cement block sheds, they're reasonably safe from Thread though food resources may have to be augmented from our supplies."

"They may have to come north in the end if we can't supply them from our

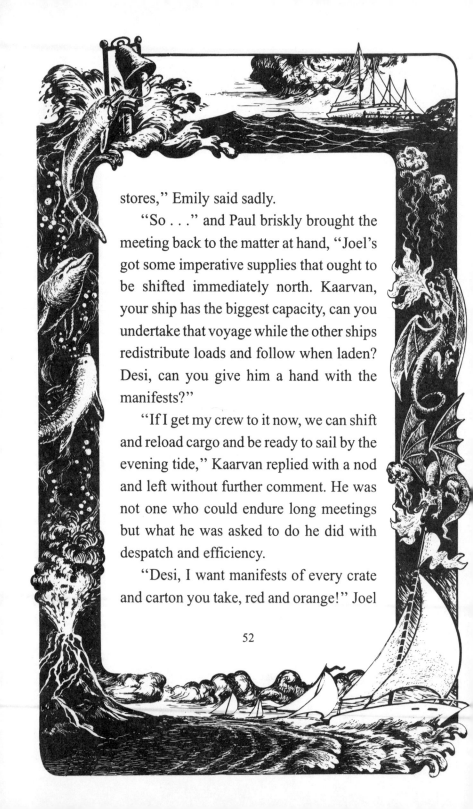

stores," Emily said sadly.

"So . . ." and Paul briskly brought the meeting back to the matter at hand, "Joel's got some imperative supplies that ought to be shifted immediately north. Kaarvan, your ship has the biggest capacity, can you undertake that voyage while the other ships redistribute loads and follow when laden? Desi, can you give him a hand with the manifests?"

"If I get my crew to it now, we can shift and reload cargo and be ready to sail by the evening tide," Kaarvan replied with a nod and left without further comment. He was not one who could endure long meetings but what he was asked to do he did with despatch and efficiency.

"Desi, I want manifests of every crate and carton you take, red and orange!" Joel

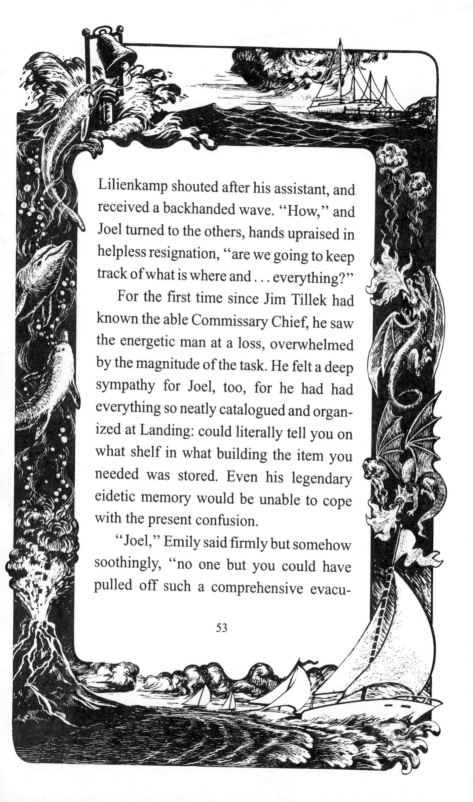

Lilienkamp shouted after his assistant, and received a backhanded wave. "How," and Joel turned to the others, hands upraised in helpless resignation, "are we going to keep track of what is where and . . . everything?"

For the first time since Jim Tillek had known the able Commissary Chief, he saw the energetic man at a loss, overwhelmed by the magnitude of the task. He felt a deep sympathy for Joel, too, for he had had everything so neatly catalogued and organized at Landing: could literally tell you on what shelf in what building the item you needed was stored. Even his legendary eidetic memory would be unable to cope with the present confusion.

"Joel," Emily said firmly but somehow soothingly, "no one but you could have pulled off such a comprehensive evacu-

53

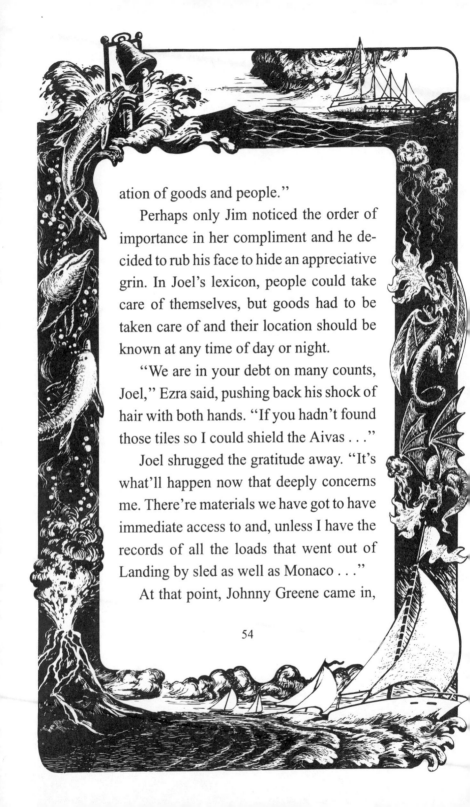

ation of goods and people."

Perhaps only Jim noticed the order of importance in her compliment and he decided to rub his face to hide an appreciative grin. In Joel's lexicon, people could take care of themselves, but goods had to be taken care of and their location should be known at any time of day or night.

"We are in your debt on many counts, Joel," Ezra said, pushing back his shock of hair with both hands. "If you hadn't found those tiles so I could shield the Aivas . . ."

Joel shrugged the gratitude away. "It's what'll happen now that deeply concerns me. There're materials we have got to have immediate access to and, unless I have the records of all the loads that went out of Landing by sled as well as Monaco . . ."

At that point, Johnny Greene came in,

54

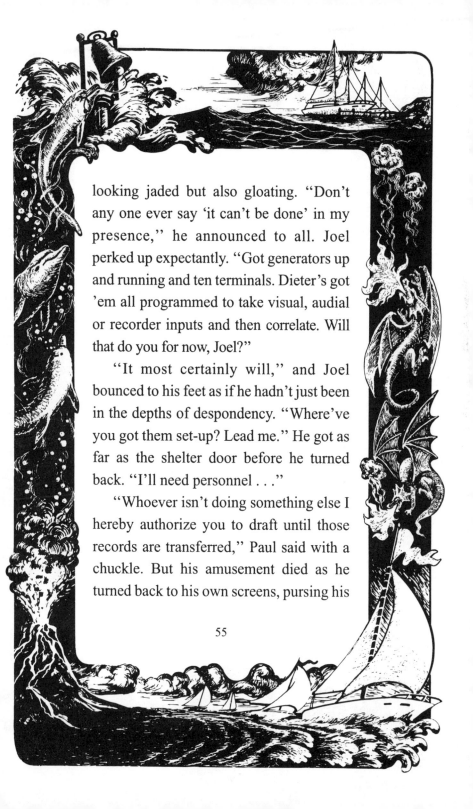

looking jaded but also gloating. "Don't any one ever say 'it can't be done' in my presence," he announced to all. Joel perked up expectantly. "Got generators up and running and ten terminals. Dieter's got 'em all programmed to take visual, audial or recorder inputs and then correlate. Will that do you for now, Joel?"

"It most certainly will," and Joel bounced to his feet as if he hadn't just been in the depths of despondency. "Where've you got them set-up? Lead me." He got as far as the shelter door before he turned back. "I'll need personnel . . ."

"Whoever isn't doing something else I hereby authorize you to draft until those records are transferred," Paul said with a chuckle. But his amusement died as he turned back to his own screens, pursing his

55

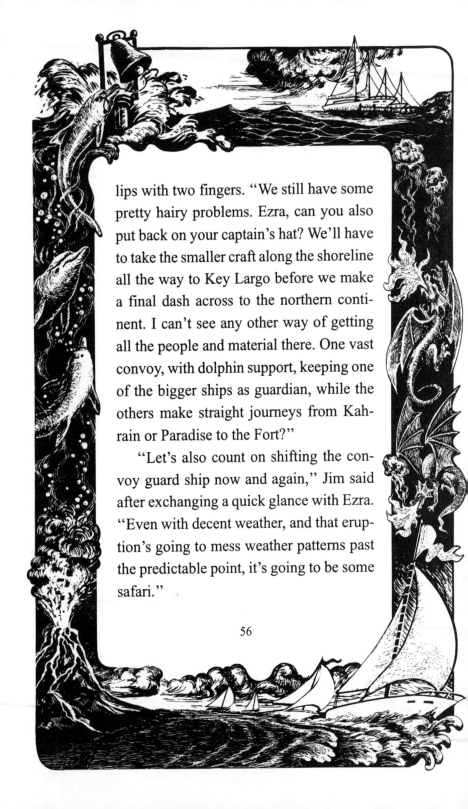

lips with two fingers. "We still have some pretty hairy problems. Ezra, can you also put back on your captain's hat? We'll have to take the smaller craft along the shoreline all the way to Key Largo before we make a final dash across to the northern continent. I can't see any other way of getting all the people and material there. One vast convoy, with dolphin support, keeping one of the bigger ships as guardian, while the others make straight journeys from Kahrain or Paradise to the Fort?"

"Let's also count on shifting the convoy guard ship now and again," Jim said after exchanging a quick glance with Ezra. "Even with decent weather, and that eruption's going to mess weather patterns past the predictable point, it's going to be some safari."

56

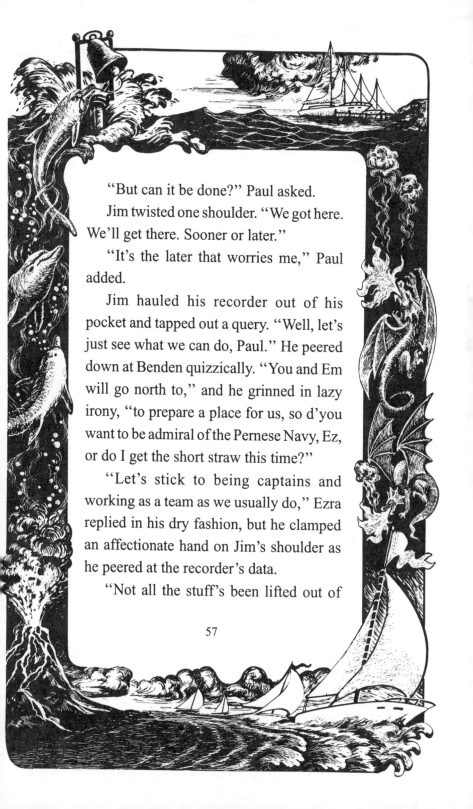

"But can it be done?" Paul asked.

Jim twisted one shoulder. "We got here. We'll get there. Sooner or later."

"It's the later that worries me," Paul added.

Jim hauled his recorder out of his pocket and tapped out a query. "Well, let's just see what we can do, Paul." He peered down at Benden quizzically. "You and Em will go north to," and he grinned in lazy irony, "to prepare a place for us, so d'you want to be admiral of the Pernese Navy, Ez, or do I get the short straw this time?"

"Let's stick to being captains and working as a team as we usually do," Ezra replied in his dry fashion, but he clamped an affectionate hand on Jim's shoulder as he peered at the recorder's data.

"Not all the stuff's been lifted out of

57

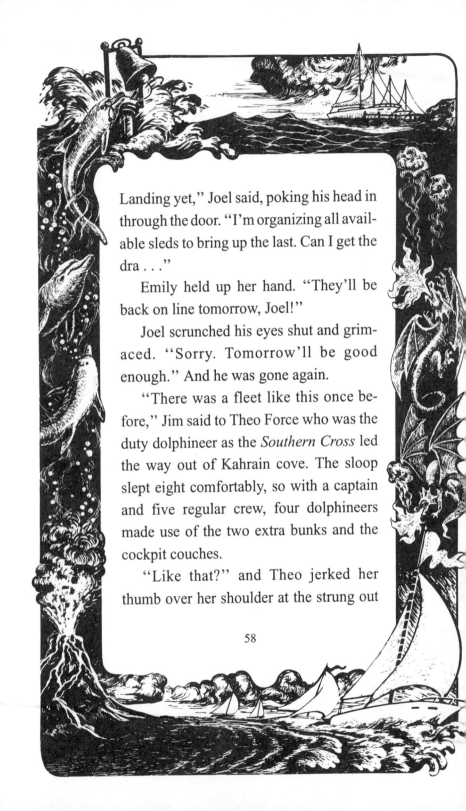

Landing yet," Joel said, poking his head in through the door. "I'm organizing all available sleds to bring up the last. Can I get the dra . . ."

Emily held up her hand. "They'll be back on line tomorrow, Joel!"

Joel scrunched his eyes shut and grimaced. "Sorry. Tomorrow'll be good enough." And he was gone again.

"There was a fleet like this once before," Jim said to Theo Force who was the duty dolphineer as the *Southern Cross* led the way out of Kahrain cove. The sloop slept eight comfortably, so with a captain and five regular crew, four dolphineers made use of the two extra bunks and the cockpit couches.

"Like that?" and Theo jerked her thumb over her shoulder at the strung out

58

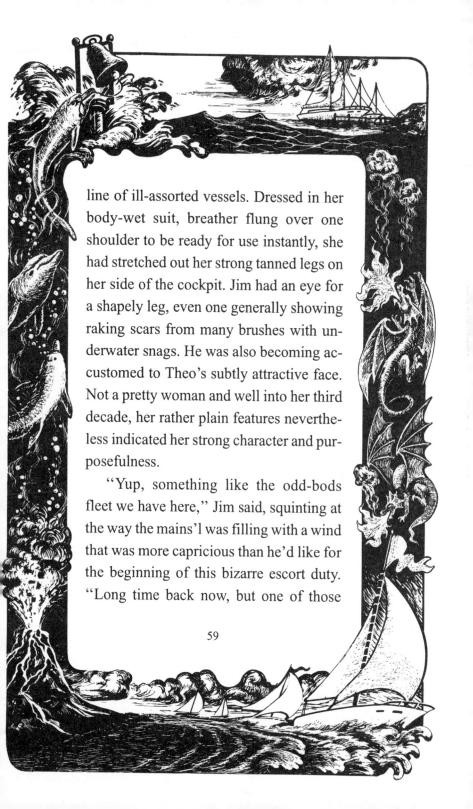

line of ill-assorted vessels. Dressed in her body-wet suit, breather flung over one shoulder to be ready for use instantly, she had stretched out her strong tanned legs on her side of the cockpit. Jim had an eye for a shapely leg, even one generally showing raking scars from many brushes with underwater snags. He was also becoming accustomed to Theo's subtly attractive face. Not a pretty woman and well into her third decade, her rather plain features nevertheless indicated her strong character and purposefulness.

"Yup, something like the odd-bods fleet we have here," Jim said, squinting at the way the mains'l was filling with a wind that was more capricious than he'd like for the beginning of this bizarre escort duty. "Long time back now, but one of those

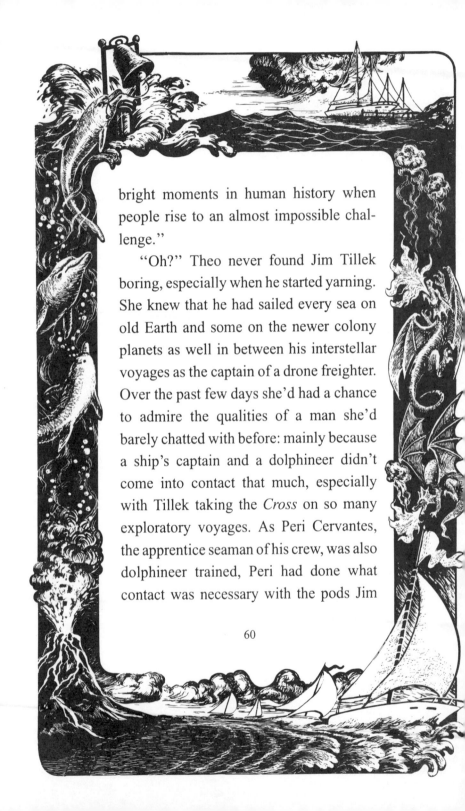

bright moments in human history when people rise to an almost impossible challenge.''

"Oh?'' Theo never found Jim Tillek boring, especially when he started yarning. She knew that he had sailed every sea on old Earth and some on the newer colony planets as well in between his interstellar voyages as the captain of a drone freighter. Over the past few days she'd had a chance to admire the qualities of a man she'd barely chatted with before: mainly because a ship's captain and a dolphineer didn't come into contact that much, especially with Tillek taking the *Cross* on so many exploratory voyages. As Peri Cervantes, the apprentice seaman of his crew, was also dolphineer trained, Peri had done what contact was necessary with the pods Jim

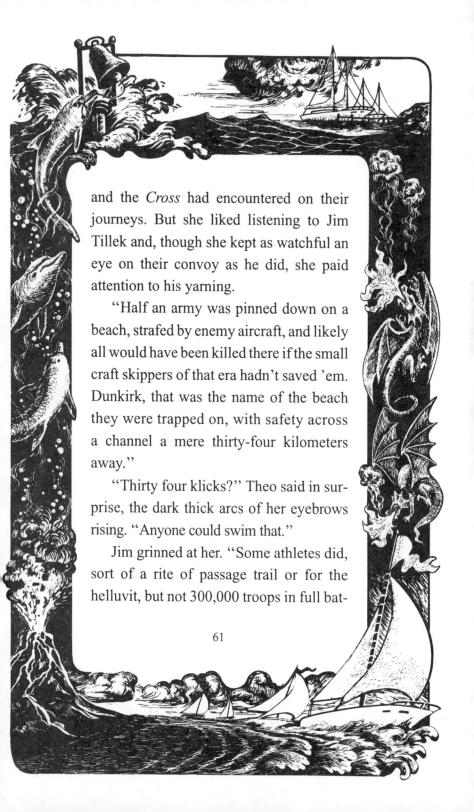

and the *Cross* had encountered on their journeys. But she liked listening to Jim Tillek and, though she kept as watchful an eye on their convoy as he did, she paid attention to his yarning.

"Half an army was pinned down on a beach, strafed by enemy aircraft, and likely all would have been killed there if the small craft skippers of that era hadn't saved 'em. Dunkirk, that was the name of the beach they were trapped on, with safety across a channel a mere thirty-four kilometers away."

"Thirty four klicks?" Theo said in surprise, the dark thick arcs of her eyebrows rising. "Anyone could swim that."

Jim grinned at her. "Some athletes did, sort of a rite of passage trail or for the helluvit, but not 300,000 troops in full bat-

61

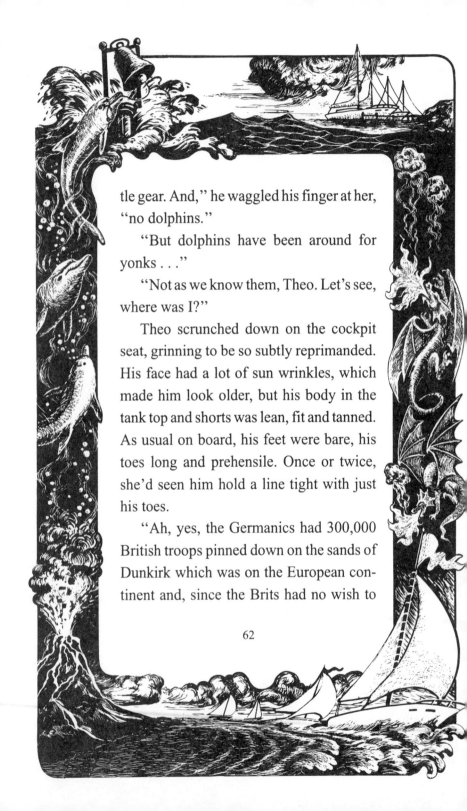

tle gear. And," he waggled his finger at her, "no dolphins."

"But dolphins have been around for yonks . . ."

"Not as we know them, Theo. Let's see, where was I?"

Theo scrunched down on the cockpit seat, grinning to be so subtly reprimanded. His face had a lot of sun wrinkles, which made him look older, but his body in the tank top and shorts was lean, fit and tanned. As usual on board, his feet were bare, his toes long and prehensile. Once or twice, she'd seen him hold a line tight with just his toes.

"Ah, yes, the Germanics had 300,000 British troops pinned down on the sands of Dunkirk which was on the European continent and, since the Brits had no wish to

62

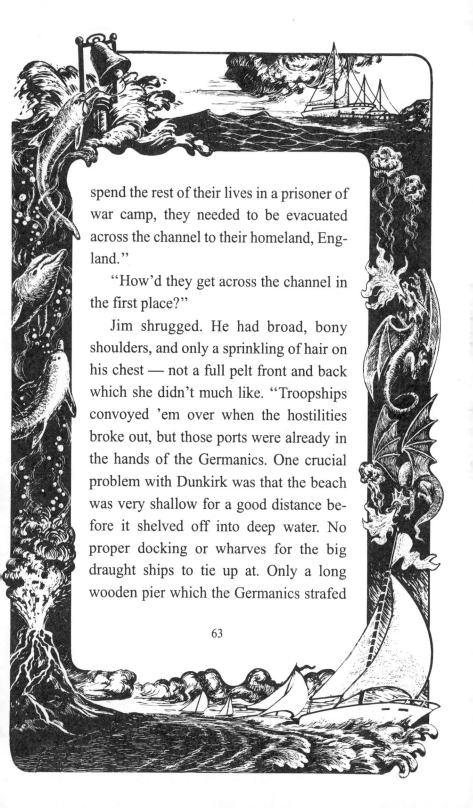

spend the rest of their lives in a prisoner of war camp, they needed to be evacuated across the channel to their homeland, England."

"How'd they get across the channel in the first place?"

Jim shrugged. He had broad, bony shoulders, and only a sprinkling of hair on his chest — not a full pelt front and back which she didn't much like. "Troopships convoyed 'em over when the hostilities broke out, but those ports were already in the hands of the Germanics. One crucial problem with Dunkirk was that the beach was very shallow for a good distance before it shelved off into deep water. No proper docking or wharves for the big draught ships to tie up at. Only a long wooden pier which the Germanics strafed

63

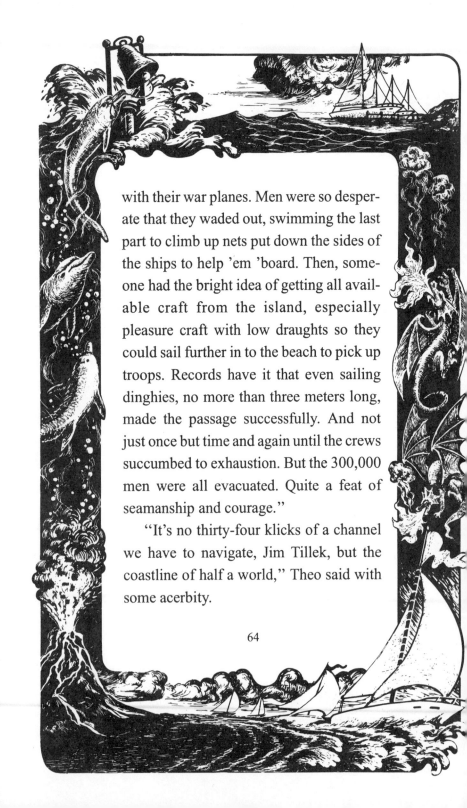

with their war planes. Men were so desperate that they waded out, swimming the last part to climb up nets put down the sides of the ships to help 'em 'board. Then, someone had the bright idea of getting all available craft from the island, especially pleasure craft with low draughts so they could sail further in to the beach to pick up troops. Records have it that even sailing dinghies, no more than three meters long, made the passage successfully. And not just once but time and again until the crews succumbed to exhaustion. But the 300,000 men were all evacuated. Quite a feat of seamanship and courage."

"It's no thirty-four klicks of a channel we have to navigate, Jim Tillek, but the coastline of half a world," Theo said with some acerbity.

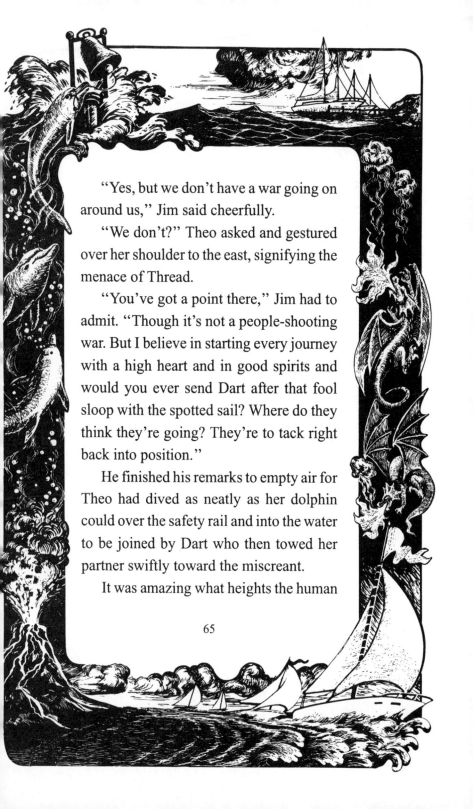

"Yes, but we don't have a war going on around us," Jim said cheerfully.

"We don't?" Theo asked and gestured over her shoulder to the east, signifying the menace of Thread.

"You've got a point there," Jim had to admit. "Though it's not a people-shooting war. But I believe in starting every journey with a high heart and in good spirits and would you ever send Dart after that fool sloop with the spotted sail? Where do they think they're going? They're to tack right back into position."

He finished his remarks to empty air for Theo had dived as neatly as her dolphin could over the safety rail and into the water to be joined by Dart who then towed her partner swiftly toward the miscreant.

It was amazing what heights the human

65

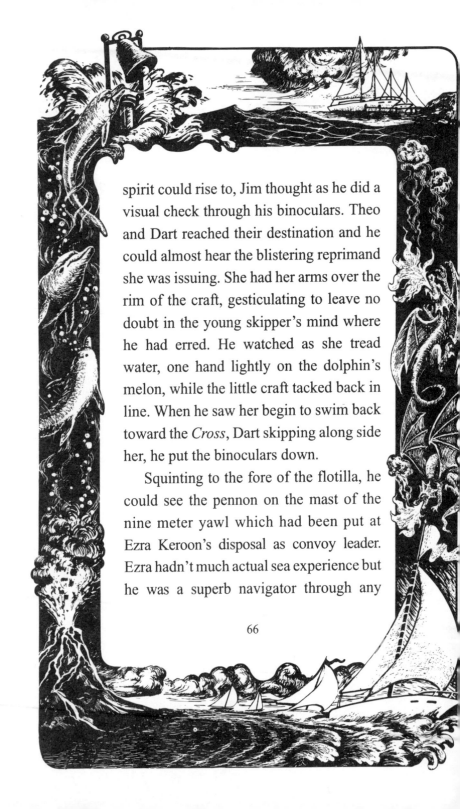

spirit could rise to, Jim thought as he did a visual check through his binoculars. Theo and Dart reached their destination and he could almost hear the blistering reprimand she was issuing. She had her arms over the rim of the craft, gesticulating to leave no doubt in the young skipper's mind where he had erred. He watched as she tread water, one hand lightly on the dolphin's melon, while the little craft tacked back in line. When he saw her begin to swim back toward the *Cross*, Dart skipping along side her, he put the binoculars down.

Squinting to the fore of the flotilla, he could see the pennon on the mast of the nine meter yawl which had been put at Ezra Keroon's disposal as convoy leader. Ezra hadn't much actual sea experience but he was a superb navigator through any

66

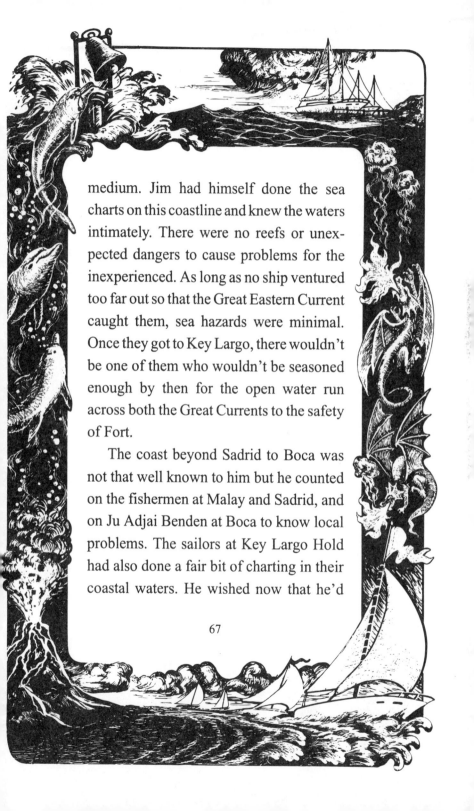

medium. Jim had himself done the sea charts on this coastline and knew the waters intimately. There were no reefs or unexpected dangers to cause problems for the inexperienced. As long as no ship ventured too far out so that the Great Eastern Current caught them, sea hazards were minimal. Once they got to Key Largo, there wouldn't be one of them who wouldn't be seasoned enough by then for the open water run across both the Great Currents to the safety of Fort.

The coast beyond Sadrid to Boca was not that well known to him but he counted on the fishermen at Malay and Sadrid, and on Ju Adjai Benden at Boca to know local problems. The sailors at Key Largo Hold had also done a fair bit of charting in their coastal waters. He wished now that he'd

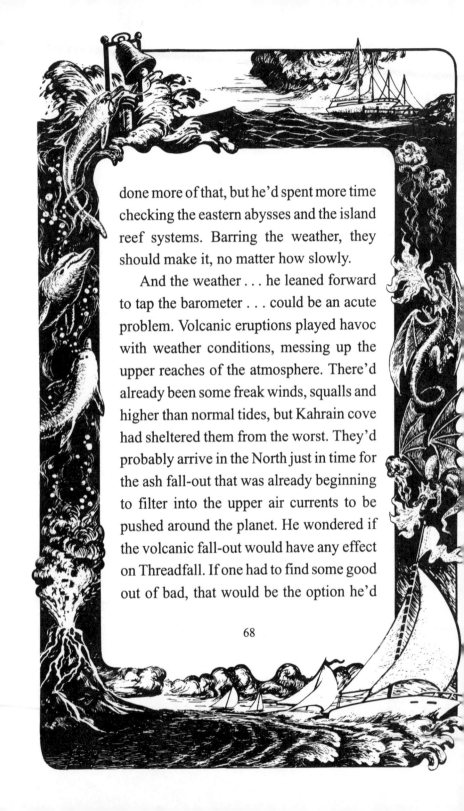

done more of that, but he'd spent more time checking the eastern abysses and the island reef systems. Barring the weather, they should make it, no matter how slowly.

And the weather . . . he leaned forward to tap the barometer . . . could be an acute problem. Volcanic eruptions played havoc with weather conditions, messing up the upper reaches of the atmosphere. There'd already been some freak winds, squalls and higher than normal tides, but Kahrain cove had sheltered them from the worst. They'd probably arrive in the North just in time for the ash fall-out that was already beginning to filter into the upper air currents to be pushed around the planet. He wondered if the volcanic fall-out would have any effect on Threadfall. If one had to find some good out of bad, that would be the option he'd

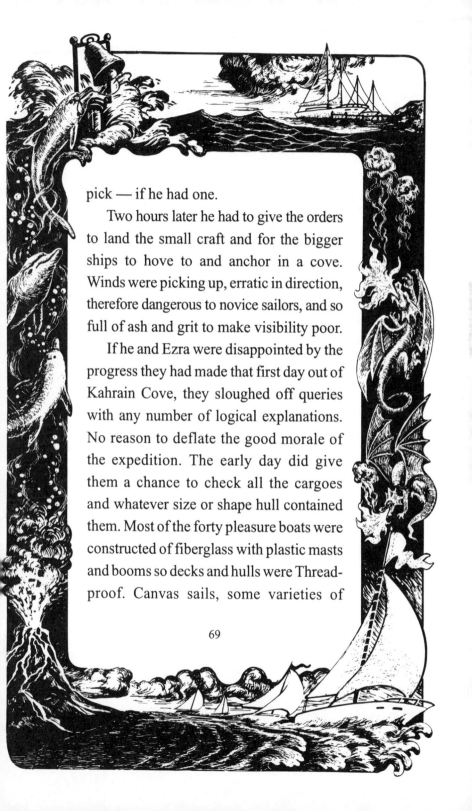

pick — if he had one.

Two hours later he had to give the orders to land the small craft and for the bigger ships to hove to and anchor in a cove. Winds were picking up, erratic in direction, therefore dangerous to novice sailors, and so full of ash and grit to make visibility poor.

If he and Ezra were disappointed by the progress they had made that first day out of Kahrain Cove, they sloughed off queries with any number of logical explanations. No reason to deflate the good morale of the expedition. The early day did give them a chance to check all the cargoes and whatever size or shape hull contained them. Most of the forty pleasure boats were constructed of fiberglass with plastic masts and booms so decks and hulls were Thread-proof. Canvas sails, some varieties of

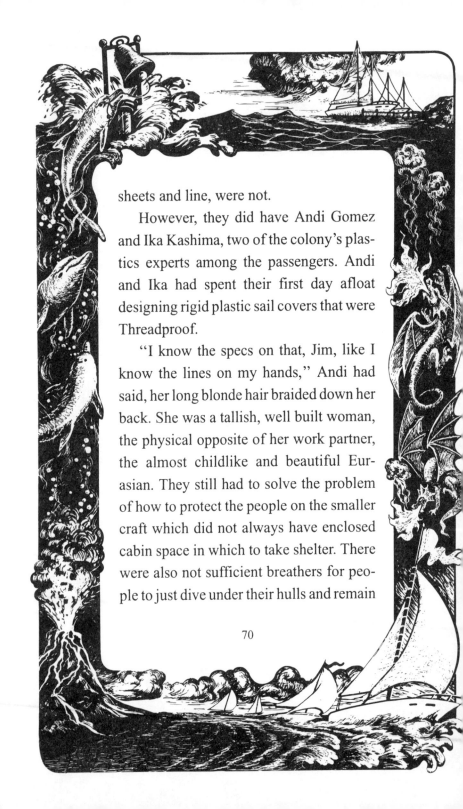

sheets and line, were not.

However, they did have Andi Gomez and Ika Kashima, two of the colony's plastics experts among the passengers. Andi and Ika had spent their first day afloat designing rigid plastic sail covers that were Threadproof.

"I know the specs on that, Jim, like I know the lines on my hands," Andi had said, her long blonde hair braided down her back. She was a tallish, well built woman, the physical opposite of her work partner, the almost childlike and beautiful Eurasian. They still had to solve the problem of how to protect the people on the smaller craft which did not always have enclosed cabin space in which to take shelter. There were also not sufficient breathers for people to just dive under their hulls and remain

70

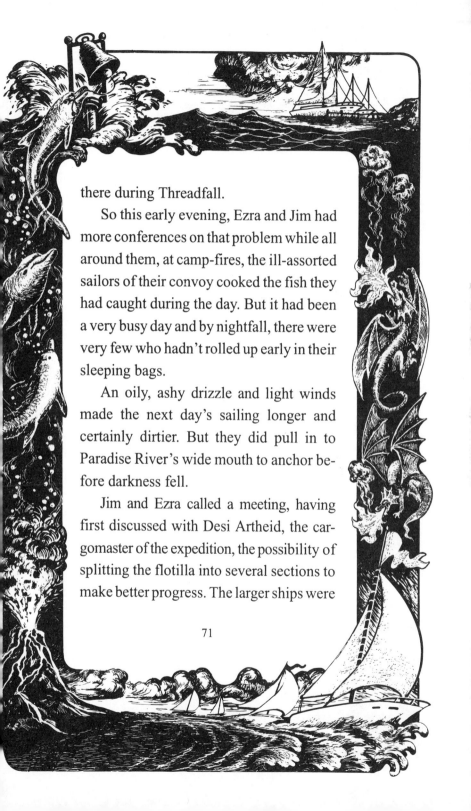

there during Threadfall.

So this early evening, Ezra and Jim had more conferences on that problem while all around them, at camp-fires, the ill-assorted sailors of their convoy cooked the fish they had caught during the day. But it had been a very busy day and by nightfall, there were very few who hadn't rolled up early in their sleeping bags.

An oily, ashy drizzle and light winds made the next day's sailing longer and certainly dirtier. But they did pull in to Paradise River's wide mouth to anchor before darkness fell.

Jim and Ezra called a meeting, having first discussed with Desi Artheid, the cargomaster of the expedition, the possibility of splitting the flotilla into several sections to make better progress. The larger ships were

71

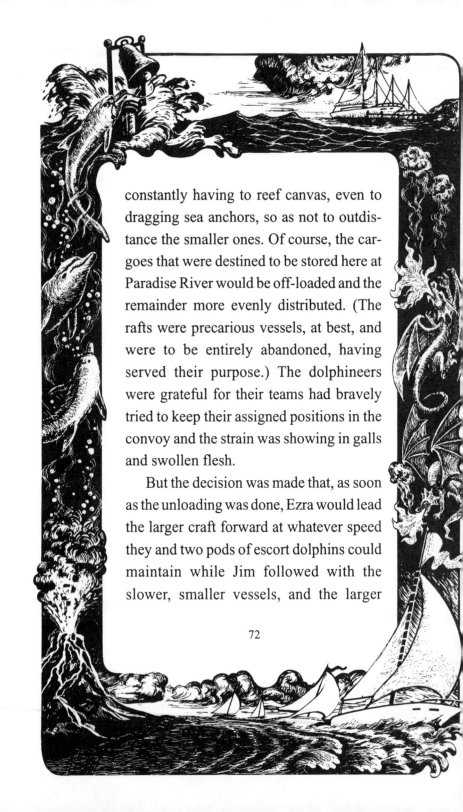

constantly having to reef canvas, even to dragging sea anchors, so as not to outdistance the smaller ones. Of course, the cargoes that were destined to be stored here at Paradise River would be off-loaded and the remainder more evenly distributed. (The rafts were precarious vessels, at best, and were to be entirely abandoned, having served their purpose.) The dolphineers were grateful for their teams had bravely tried to keep their assigned positions in the convoy and the strain was showing in galls and swollen flesh.

But the decision was made that, as soon as the unloading was done, Ezra would lead the larger craft forward at whatever speed they and two pods of escort dolphins could maintain while Jim followed with the slower, smaller vessels, and the larger

72

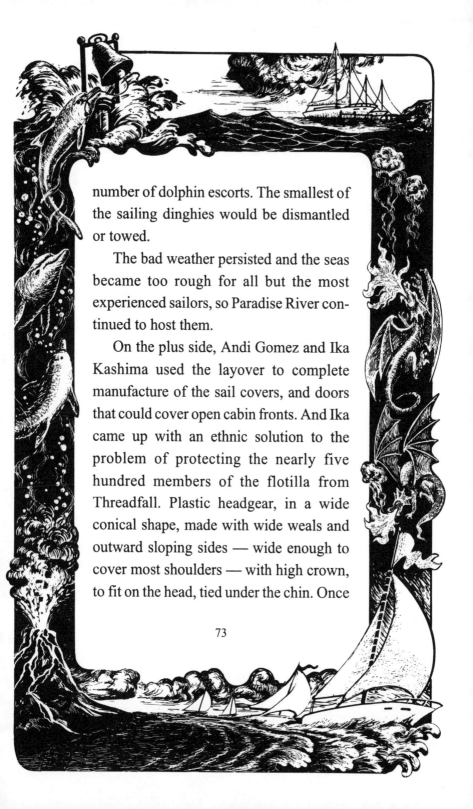

number of dolphin escorts. The smallest of the sailing dinghies would be dismantled or towed.

The bad weather persisted and the seas became too rough for all but the most experienced sailors, so Paradise River continued to host them.

On the plus side, Andi Gomez and Ika Kashima used the layover to complete manufacture of the sail covers, and doors that could cover open cabin fronts. And Ika came up with an ethnic solution to the problem of protecting the nearly five hundred members of the flotilla from Threadfall. Plastic headgear, in a wide conical shape, made with wide weals and outward sloping sides — wide enough to cover most shoulders — with high crown, to fit on the head, tied under the chin. Once

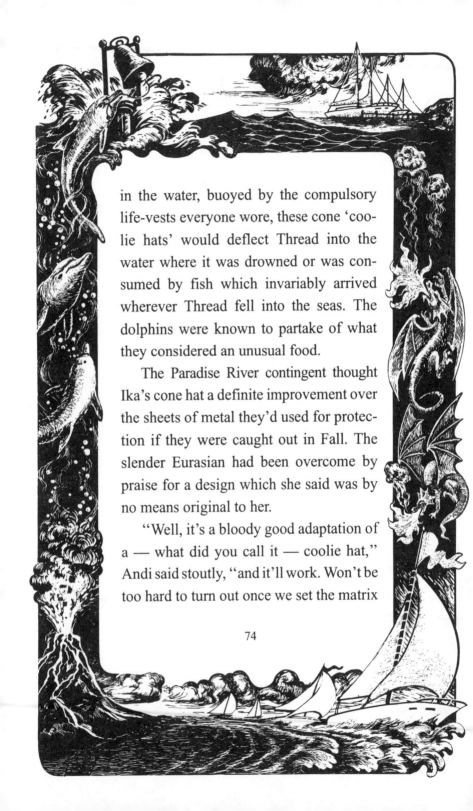

in the water, buoyed by the compulsory life-vests everyone wore, these cone 'coolie hats' would deflect Thread into the water where it was drowned or was consumed by fish which invariably arrived wherever Thread fell into the seas. The dolphins were known to partake of what they considered an unusual food.

The Paradise River contingent thought Ika's cone hat a definite improvement over the sheets of metal they'd used for protection if they were caught out in Fall. The slender Eurasian had been overcome by praise for a design which she said was by no means original to her.

"Well, it's a bloody good adaptation of a — what did you call it — coolie hat," Andi said stoutly, "and it'll work. Won't be too hard to turn out once we set the matrix

74

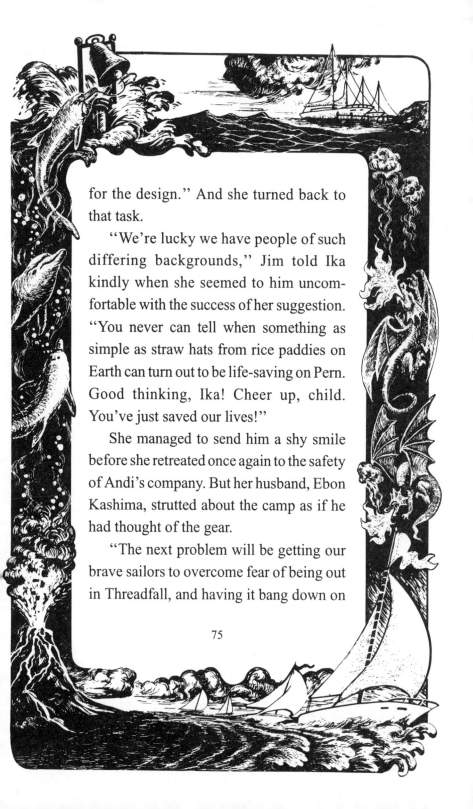

for the design." And she turned back to that task.

"We're lucky we have people of such differing backgrounds," Jim told Ika kindly when she seemed to him uncomfortable with the success of her suggestion. "You never can tell when something as simple as straw hats from rice paddies on Earth can turn out to be life-saving on Pern. Good thinking, Ika! Cheer up, child. You've just saved our lives!"

She managed to send him a shy smile before she retreated once again to the safety of Andi's company. But her husband, Ebon Kashima, strutted about the camp as if he had thought of the gear.

"The next problem will be getting our brave sailors to overcome fear of being out in Threadfall, and having it bang down on

75

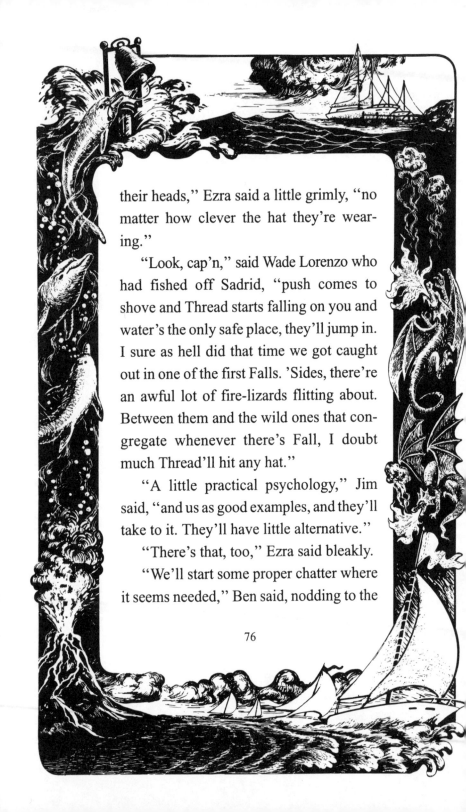

their heads," Ezra said a little grimly, "no matter how clever the hat they're wearing."

"Look, cap'n," said Wade Lorenzo who had fished off Sadrid, "push comes to shove and Thread starts falling on you and water's the only safe place, they'll jump in. I sure as hell did that time we got caught out in one of the first Falls. 'Sides, there're an awful lot of fire-lizards flitting about. Between them and the wild ones that congregate whenever there's Fall, I doubt much Thread'll hit any hat."

"A little practical psychology," Jim said, "and us as good examples, and they'll take to it. They'll have little alternative."

"There's that, too," Ezra said bleakly.

"We'll start some proper chatter where it seems needed," Ben said, nodding to the

76

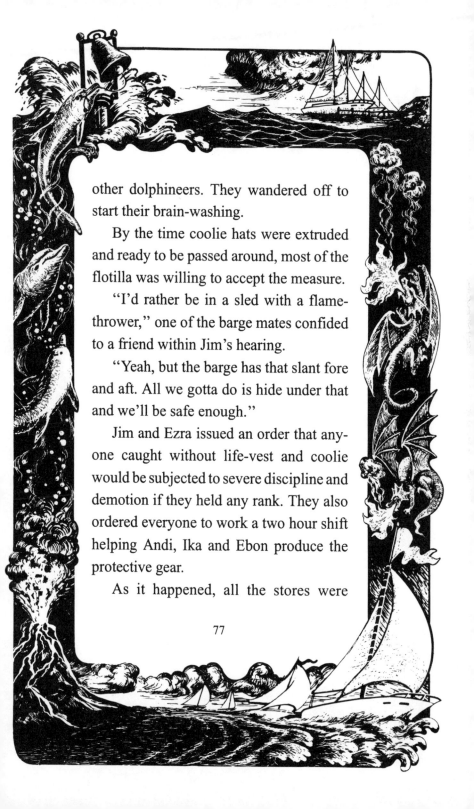

other dolphineers. They wandered off to start their brain-washing.

By the time coolie hats were extruded and ready to be passed around, most of the flotilla was willing to accept the measure.

"I'd rather be in a sled with a flame-thrower," one of the barge mates confided to a friend within Jim's hearing.

"Yeah, but the barge has that slant fore and aft. All we gotta do is hide under that and we'll be safe enough."

Jim and Ezra issued an order that any-one caught without life-vest and coolie would be subjected to severe discipline and demotion if they held any rank. They also ordered everyone to work a two hour shift helping Andi, Ika and Ebon produce the protective gear.

As it happened, all the stores were

77

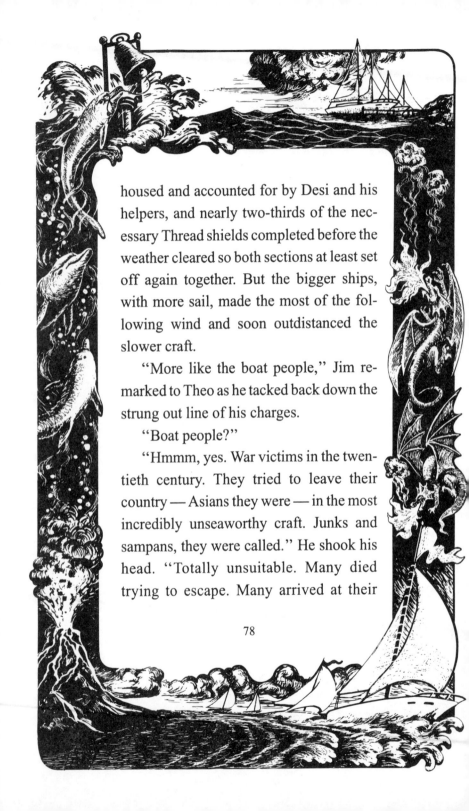

housed and accounted for by Desi and his helpers, and nearly two-thirds of the necessary Thread shields completed before the weather cleared so both sections at least set off again together. But the bigger ships, with more sail, made the most of the following wind and soon outdistanced the slower craft.

"More like the boat people," Jim remarked to Theo as he tacked back down the strung out line of his charges.

"Boat people?"

"Hmmm, yes. War victims in the twentieth century. They tried to leave their country — Asians they were — in the most incredibly unseaworthy craft. Junks and sampans, they were called." He shook his head. "Totally unsuitable. Many died trying to escape. Many arrived at their

78

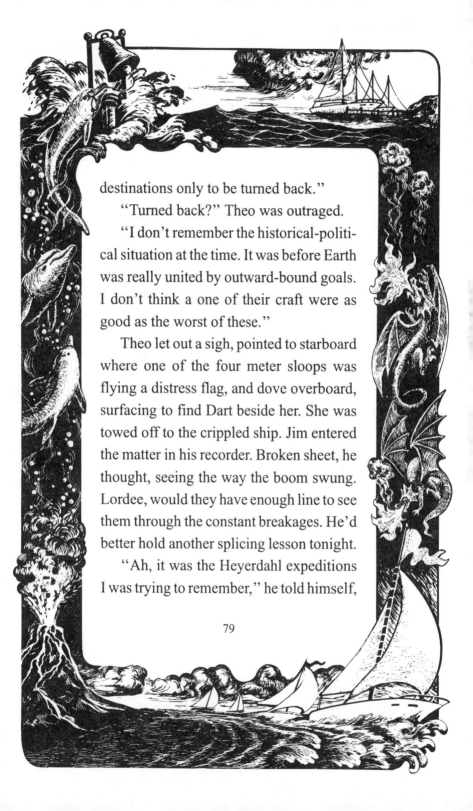

destinations only to be turned back."

"Turned back?" Theo was outraged.

"I don't remember the historical-political situation at the time. It was before Earth was really united by outward-bound goals. I don't think a one of their craft were as good as the worst of these."

Theo let out a sigh, pointed to starboard where one of the four meter sloops was flying a distress flag, and dove overboard, surfacing to find Dart beside her. She was towed off to the crippled ship. Jim entered the matter in his recorder. Broken sheet, he thought, seeing the way the boom swung. Lordee, would they have enough line to see them through the constant breakages. He'd better hold another splicing lesson tonight.

"Ah, it was the Heyerdahl expeditions I was trying to remember," he told himself,

79

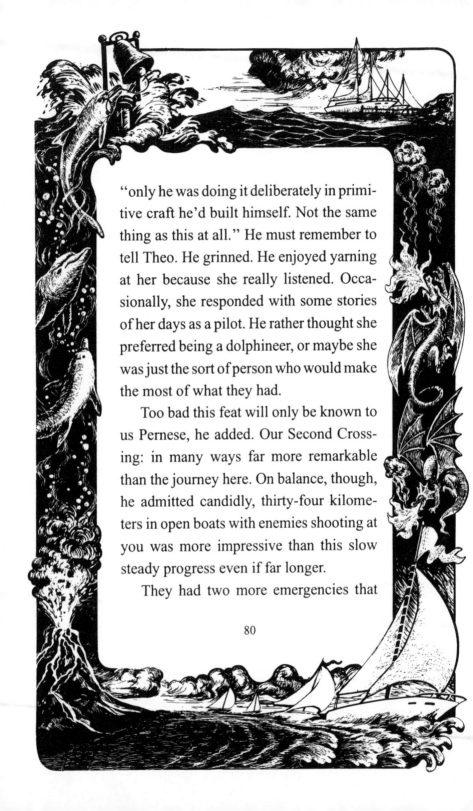

"only he was doing it deliberately in primitive craft he'd built himself. Not the same thing as this at all." He must remember to tell Theo. He grinned. He enjoyed yarning at her because she really listened. Occasionally, she responded with some stories of her days as a pilot. He rather thought she preferred being a dolphineer, or maybe she was just the sort of person who would make the most of what they had.

Too bad this feat will only be known to us Pernese, he added. Our Second Crossing: in many ways far more remarkable than the journey here. On balance, though, he admitted candidly, thirty-four kilometers in open boats with enemies shooting at you was more impressive than this slow steady progress even if far longer.

They had two more emergencies that

80

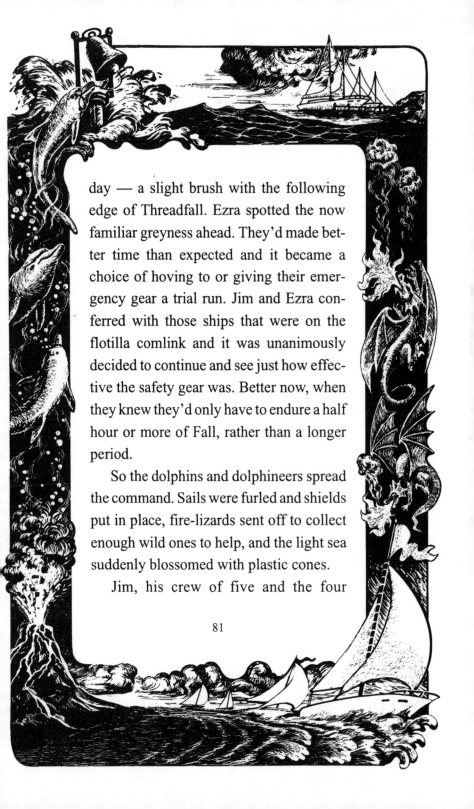

day — a slight brush with the following edge of Threadfall. Ezra spotted the now familiar greyness ahead. They'd made better time than expected and it became a choice of hoving to or giving their emergency gear a trial run. Jim and Ezra conferred with those ships that were on the flotilla comlink and it was unanimously decided to continue and see just how effective the safety gear was. Better now, when they knew they'd only have to endure a half hour or more of Fall, rather than a longer period.

So the dolphins and dolphineers spread the command. Sails were furled and shields put in place, fire-lizards sent off to collect enough wild ones to help, and the light sea suddenly blossomed with plastic cones.

Jim, his crew of five and the four

81

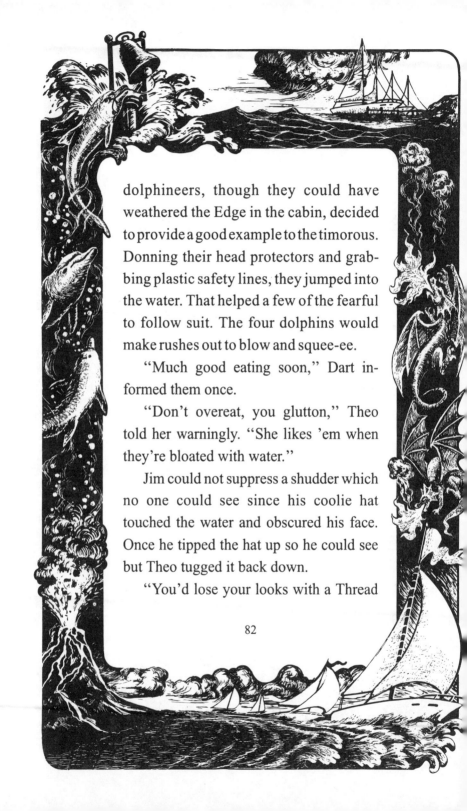

dolphineers, though they could have
weathered the Edge in the cabin, decided
to provide a good example to the timorous.
Donning their head protectors and grab-
bing plastic safety lines, they jumped into
the water. That helped a few of the fearful
to follow suit. The four dolphins would
make rushes out to blow and squee-ee.

"Much good eating soon," Dart informed them once.

"Don't overeat, you glutton," Theo
told her warningly. "She likes 'em when
they're bloated with water."

Jim could not suppress a shudder which
no one could see since his coolie hat
touched the water and obscured his face.
Once he tipped the hat up so he could see
but Theo tugged it back down.

"You'd lose your looks with a Thread

82

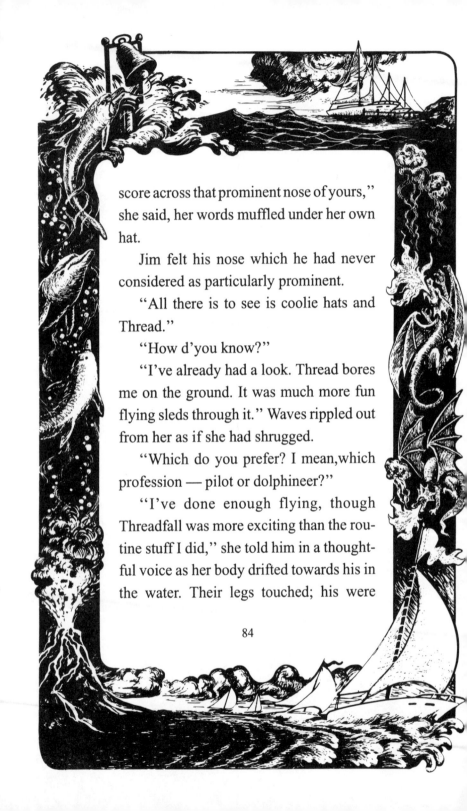

score across that prominent nose of yours,"
she said, her words muffled under her own
hat.

Jim felt his nose which he had never
considered as particularly prominent.

"All there is to see is coolie hats and
Thread."

"How d'you know?"

"I've already had a look. Thread bores
me on the ground. It was much more fun
flying sleds through it." Waves rippled out
from her as if she had shrugged.

"Which do you prefer? I mean,which
profession — pilot or dolphineer?"

"I've done enough flying, though
Threadfall was more exciting than the routine stuff I did," she told him in a thoughtful voice as her body drifted towards his in
the water. Their legs touched; his were

84

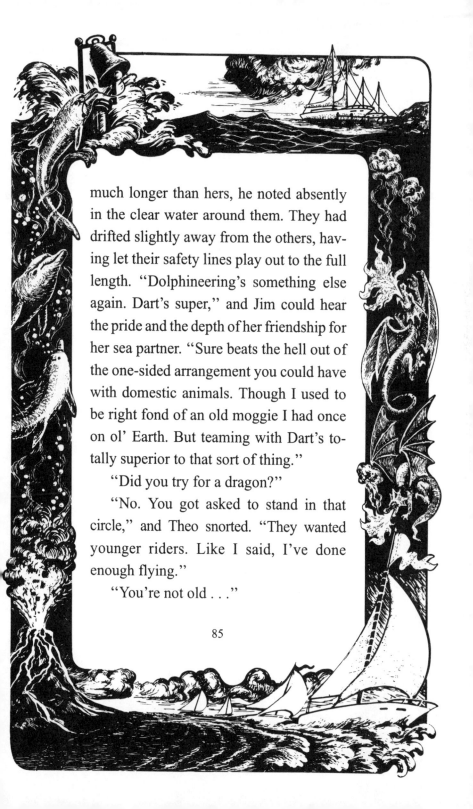

much longer than hers, he noted absently in the clear water around them. They had drifted slightly away from the others, having let their safety lines play out to the full length. "Dolphineering's something else again. Dart's super," and Jim could hear the pride and the depth of her friendship for her sea partner. "Sure beats the hell out of the one-sided arrangement you could have with domestic animals. Though I used to be right fond of an old moggie I had once on ol' Earth. But teaming with Dart's totally superior to that sort of thing."

"Did you try for a dragon?"

"No. You got asked to stand in that circle," and Theo snorted. "They wanted younger riders. Like I said, I've done enough flying."

"You're not old . . ."

85

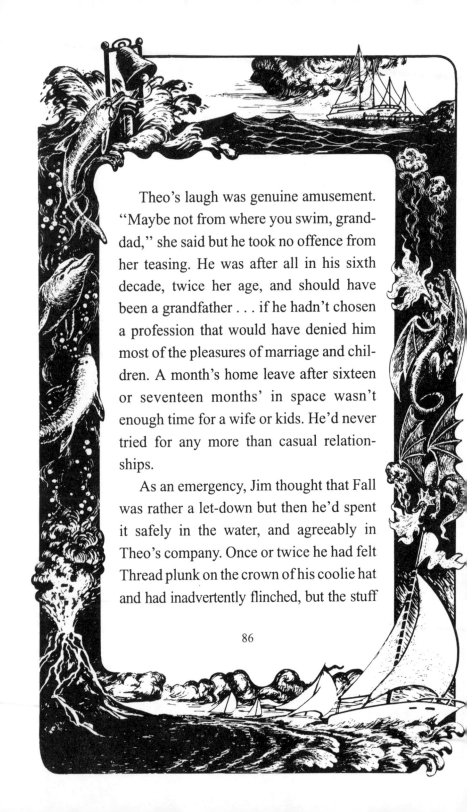

Theo's laugh was genuine amusement. "Maybe not from where you swim, granddad," she said but he took no offence from her teasing. He was after all in his sixth decade, twice her age, and should have been a grandfather . . . if he hadn't chosen a profession that would have denied him most of the pleasures of marriage and children. A month's home leave after sixteen or seventeen months' in space wasn't enough time for a wife or kids. He'd never tried for any more than casual relationships.

As an emergency, Jim thought that Fall was rather a let-down but then he'd spent it safely in the water, and agreeably in Theo's company. Once or twice he had felt Thread plunk on the crown of his coolie hat and had inadvertently flinched, but the stuff

86

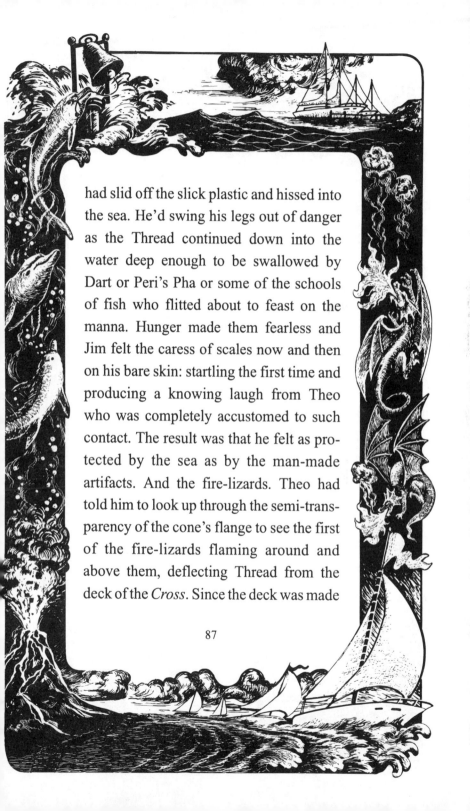

had slid off the slick plastic and hissed into the sea. He'd swing his legs out of danger as the Thread continued down into the water deep enough to be swallowed by Dart or Peri's Pha or some of the schools of fish who flitted about to feast on the manna. Hunger made them fearless and Jim felt the caress of scales now and then on his bare skin: startling the first time and producing a knowing laugh from Theo who was completely accustomed to such contact. The result was that he felt as protected by the sea as by the man-made artifacts. And the fire-lizards. Theo had told him to look up through the semi-transparency of the cone's flange to see the first of the fire-lizards flaming around and above them, deflecting Thread from the deck of the *Cross*. Since the deck was made

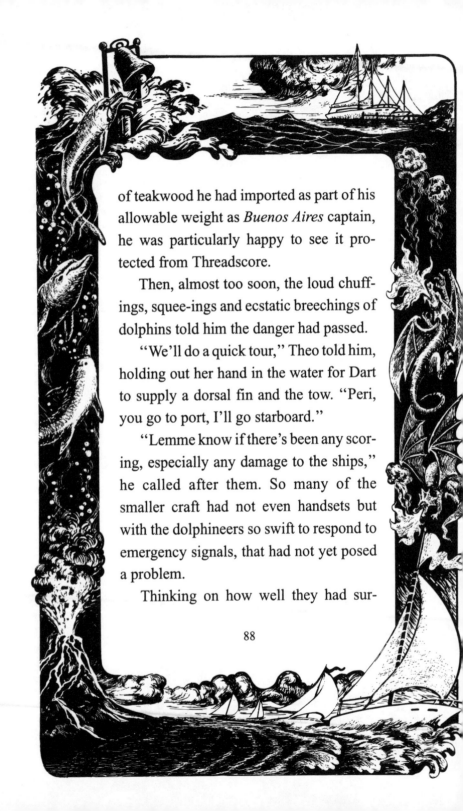

of teakwood he had imported as part of his allowable weight as *Buenos Aires* captain, he was particularly happy to see it protected from Threadscore.

Then, almost too soon, the loud chuffings, squee-ings and ecstatic breechings of dolphins told him the danger had passed.

"We'll do a quick tour," Theo told him, holding out her hand in the water for Dart to supply a dorsal fin and the tow. "Peri, you go to port, I'll go starboard."

"Lemme know if there's been any scoring, especially any damage to the ships," he called after them. So many of the smaller craft had not even handsets but with the dolphineers so swift to respond to emergency signals, that had not yet posed a problem.

Thinking on how well they had sur-

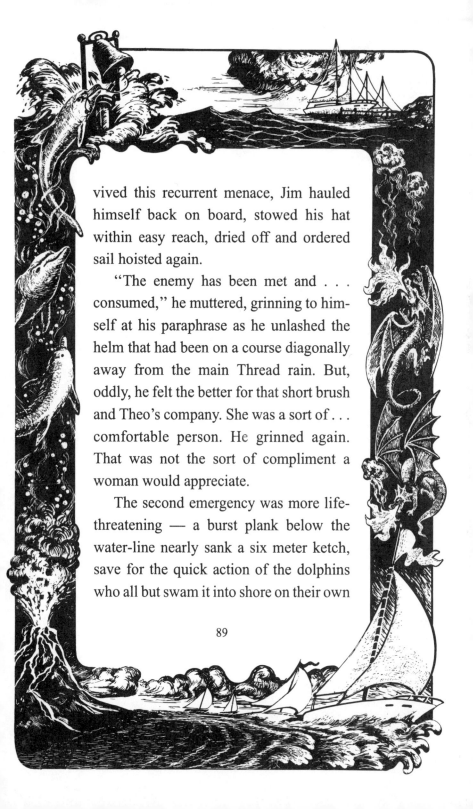

vived this recurrent menace, Jim hauled himself back on board, stowed his hat within easy reach, dried off and ordered sail hoisted again.

"The enemy has been met and . . . consumed," he muttered, grinning to himself at his paraphrase as he unlashed the helm that had been on a course diagonally away from the main Thread rain. But, oddly, he felt the better for that short brush and Theo's company. She was a sort of . . . comfortable person. He grinned again. That was not the sort of compliment a woman would appreciate.

The second emergency was more life-threatening — a burst plank below the water-line nearly sank a six meter ketch, save for the quick action of the dolphins who all but swam it into shore on their own

89

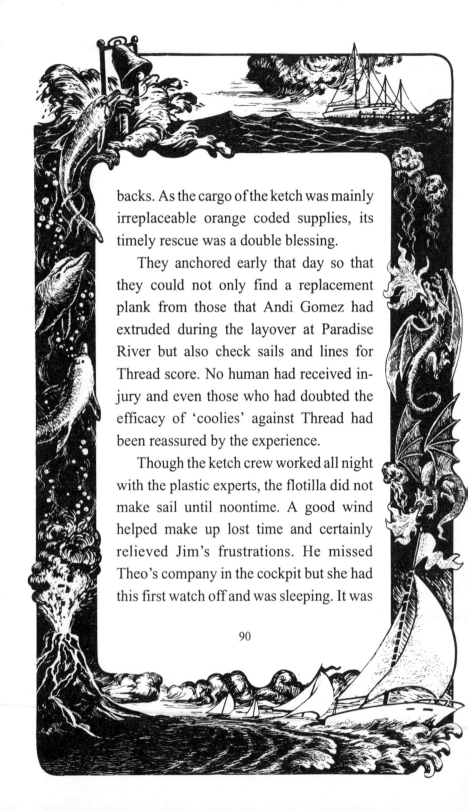

backs. As the cargo of the ketch was mainly irreplaceable orange coded supplies, its timely rescue was a double blessing.

They anchored early that day so that they could not only find a replacement plank from those that Andi Gomez had extruded during the layover at Paradise River but also check sails and lines for Thread score. No human had received injury and even those who had doubted the efficacy of 'coolies' against Thread had been reassured by the experience.

Though the ketch crew worked all night with the plastic experts, the flotilla did not make sail until noontime. A good wind helped make up lost time and certainly relieved Jim's frustrations. He missed Theo's company in the cockpit but she had this first watch off and was sleeping. It was

90

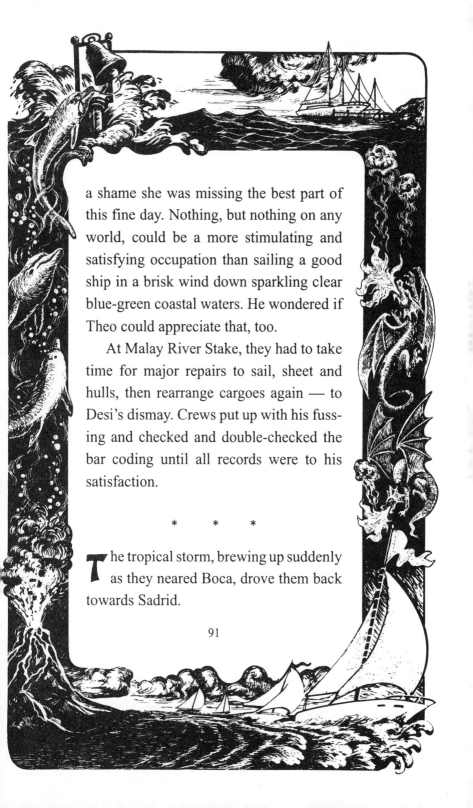

a shame she was missing the best part of this fine day. Nothing, but nothing on any world, could be a more stimulating and satisfying occupation than sailing a good ship in a brisk wind down sparkling clear blue-green coastal waters. He wondered if Theo could appreciate that, too.

At Malay River Stake, they had to take time for major repairs to sail, sheet and hulls, then rearrange cargoes again — to Desi's dismay. Crews put up with his fussing and checked and double-checked the bar coding until all records were to his satisfaction.

\*      \*      \*

*T*he tropical storm, brewing up suddenly as they neared Boca, drove them back towards Sadrid.

91

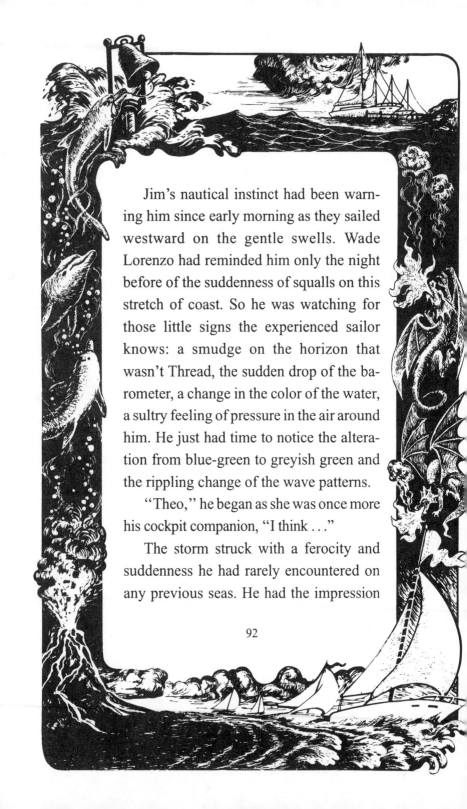

Jim's nautical instinct had been warning him since early morning as they sailed westward on the gentle swells. Wade Lorenzo had reminded him only the night before of the suddenness of squalls on this stretch of coast. So he was watching for those little signs the experienced sailor knows: a smudge on the horizon that wasn't Thread, the sudden drop of the barometer, a change in the color of the water, a sultry feeling of pressure in the air around him. He just had time to notice the alteration from blue-green to greyish green and the rippling change of the wave patterns.

"Theo," he began as she was once more his cockpit companion, "I think . . ."

The storm struck with a ferocity and suddenness he had rarely encountered on any previous seas. He had the impression

92

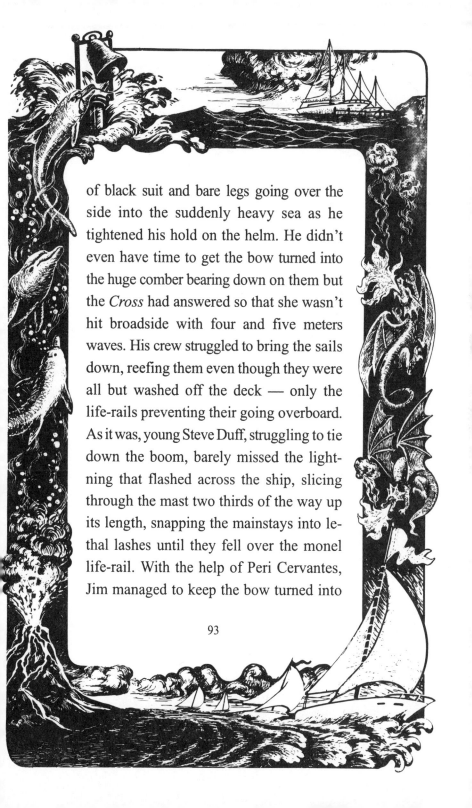

of black suit and bare legs going over the side into the suddenly heavy sea as he tightened his hold on the helm. He didn't even have time to get the bow turned into the huge comber bearing down on them but the *Cross* had answered so that she wasn't hit broadside with four and five meters waves. His crew struggled to bring the sails down, reefing them even though they were all but washed off the deck — only the life-rails preventing their going overboard. As it was, young Steve Duff, struggling to tie down the boom, barely missed the lightning that flashed across the ship, slicing through the mast two thirds of the way up its length, snapping the mainstays into lethal lashes until they fell over the monel life-rail. With the help of Peri Cervantes, Jim managed to keep the bow turned into

93

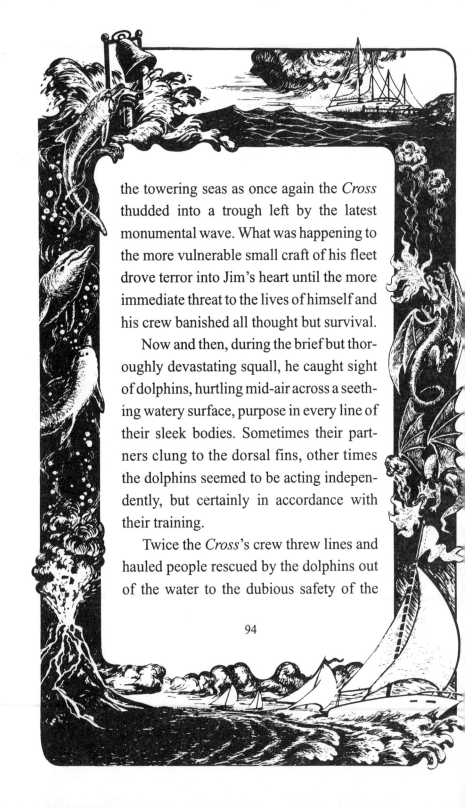

the towering seas as once again the *Cross* thudded into a trough left by the latest monumental wave. What was happening to the more vulnerable small craft of his fleet drove terror into Jim's heart until the more immediate threat to the lives of himself and his crew banished all thought but survival.

Now and then, during the brief but thoroughly devastating squall, he caught sight of dolphins, hurtling mid-air across a seething watery surface, purpose in every line of their sleek bodies. Sometimes their partners clung to the dorsal fins, other times the dolphins seemed to be acting independently, but certainly in accordance with their training.

Twice the *Cross*'s crew threw lines and hauled people rescued by the dolphins out of the water to the dubious safety of the

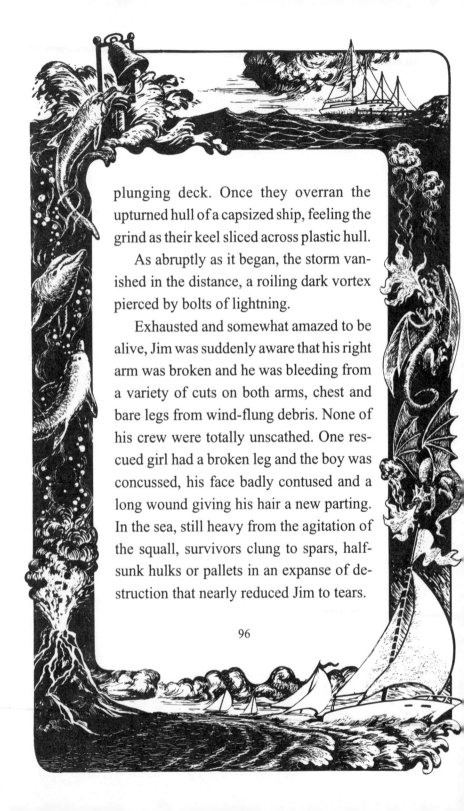

plunging deck. Once they overran the
upturned hull of a capsized ship, feeling the
grind as their keel sliced across plastic hull.

As abruptly as it began, the storm van-
ished in the distance, a roiling dark vortex
pierced by bolts of lightning.

Exhausted and somewhat amazed to be
alive, Jim was suddenly aware that his right
arm was broken and he was bleeding from
a variety of cuts on both arms, chest and
bare legs from wind-flung debris. None of
his crew were totally unscathed. One rescued girl had a broken leg and the boy was
concussed, his face badly contused and a
long wound giving his hair a new parting.
In the sea, still heavy from the agitation of
the squall, survivors clung to spars, half-
sunk hulks or pallets in an expanse of de-
struction that nearly reduced Jim to tears.

96

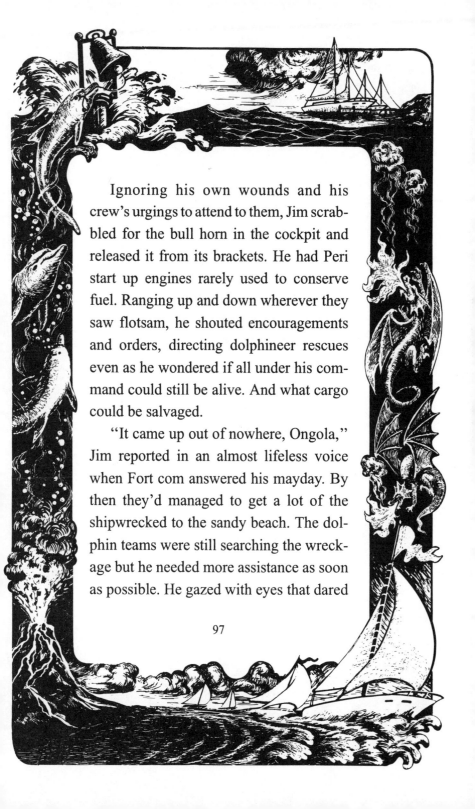

Ignoring his own wounds and his crew's urgings to attend to them, Jim scrabbled for the bull horn in the cockpit and released it from its brackets. He had Peri start up engines rarely used to conserve fuel. Ranging up and down wherever they saw flotsam, he shouted encouragements and orders, directing dolphineer rescues even as he wondered if all under his command could still be alive. And what cargo could be salvaged.

"It came up out of nowhere, Ongola," Jim reported in an almost lifeless voice when Fort com answered his mayday. By then they'd managed to get a lot of the shipwrecked to the sandy beach. The dolphin teams were still searching the wreckage but he needed more assistance as soon as possible. He gazed with eyes that dared

97

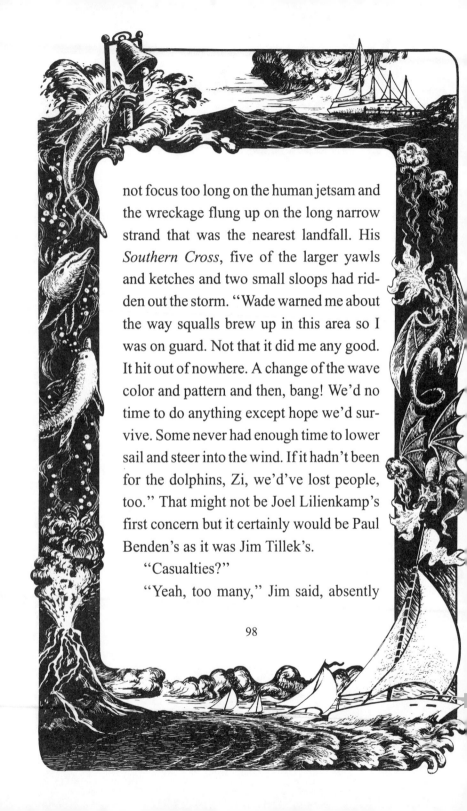

not focus too long on the human jetsam and
the wreckage flung up on the long narrow
strand that was the nearest landfall. His
*Southern Cross*, five of the larger yawls
and ketches and two small sloops had rid-
den out the storm. "Wade warned me about
the way squalls brew up in this area so I
was on guard. Not that it did me any good.
It hit out of nowhere. A change of the wave
color and pattern and then, bang! We'd no
time to do anything except hope we'd sur-
vive. Some never had enough time to lower
sail and steer into the wind. If it hadn't been
for the dolphins, Zi, we'd've lost people,
too." That might not be Joel Lilienkamp's
first concern but it certainly would be Paul
Benden's as it was Jim Tillek's.

"Casualties?"

"Yeah, too many," Jim said, absently

98

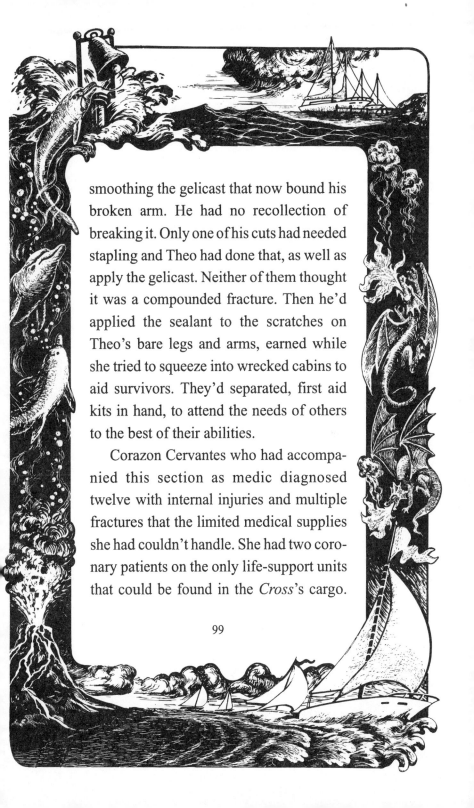

smoothing the gelicast that now bound his
broken arm. He had no recollection of
breaking it. Only one of his cuts had needed
stapling and Theo had done that, as well as
apply the gelicast. Neither of them thought
it was a compounded fracture. Then he'd
applied the sealant to the scratches on
Theo's bare legs and arms, earned while
she tried to squeeze into wrecked cabins to
aid survivors. They'd separated, first aid
kits in hand, to attend the needs of others
to the best of their abilities.

Corazon Cervantes who had accompa-
nied this section as medic diagnosed
twelve with internal injuries and multiple
fractures that the limited medical supplies
she had couldn't handle. She had two coronary patients on the only life-support units
that could be found in the *Cross*'s cargo.

99

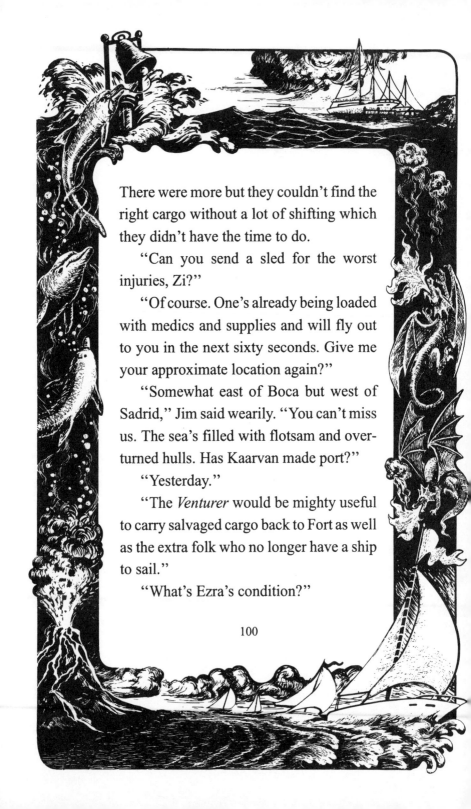

There were more but they couldn't find the right cargo without a lot of shifting which they didn't have the time to do.

"Can you send a sled for the worst injuries, Zi?"

"Of course. One's already being loaded with medics and supplies and will fly out to you in the next sixty seconds. Give me your approximate location again?"

"Somewhat east of Boca but west of Sadrid," Jim said wearily. "You can't miss us. The sea's filled with flotsam and over-turned hulls. Has Kaarvan made port?"

"Yesterday."

"The *Venturer* would be mighty useful to carry salvaged cargo back to Fort as well as the extra folk who no longer have a ship to sail."

"What's Ezra's condition?"

100

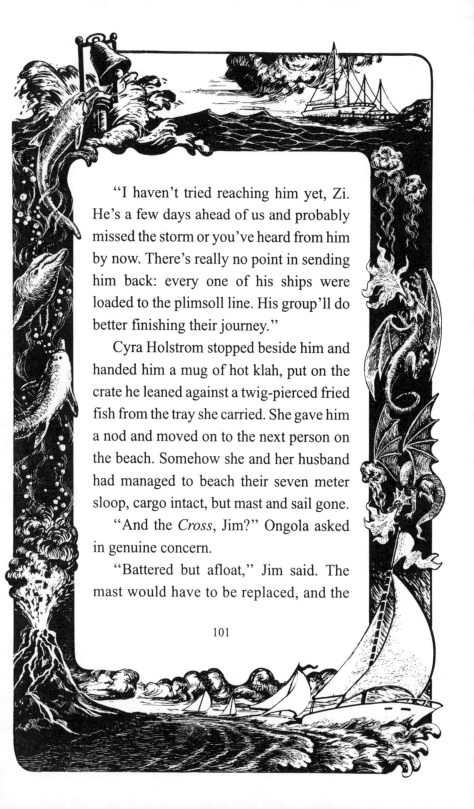

"I haven't tried reaching him yet, Zi. He's a few days ahead of us and probably missed the storm or you've heard from him by now. There's really no point in sending him back: every one of his ships were loaded to the plimsoll line. His group'll do better finishing their journey."

Cyra Holstrom stopped beside him and handed him a mug of hot klah, put on the crate he leaned against a twig-pierced fried fish from the tray she carried. She gave him a nod and moved on to the next person on the beach. Somehow she and her husband had managed to beach their seven meter sloop, cargo intact, but mast and sail gone.

"And the *Cross*, Jim?" Ongola asked in genuine concern.

"Battered but afloat," Jim said. The mast would have to be replaced, and the

101

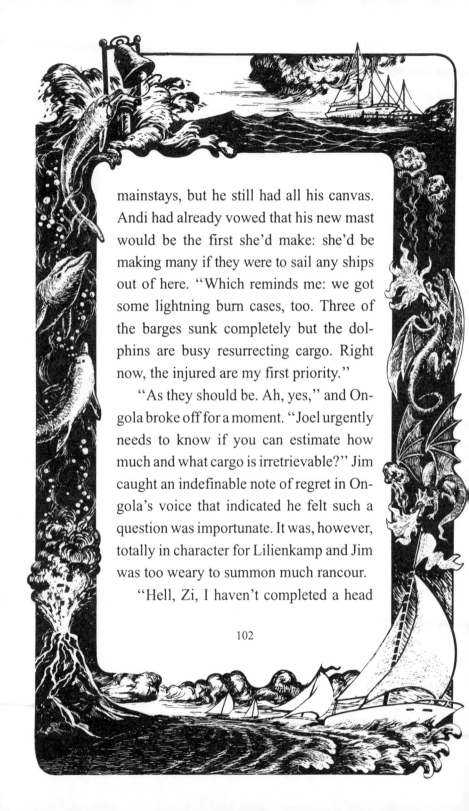

mainstays, but he still had all his canvas. Andi had already vowed that his new mast would be the first she'd make: she'd be making many if they were to sail any ships out of here. "Which reminds me: we got some lightning burn cases, too. Three of the barges sunk completely but the dolphins are busy resurrecting cargo. Right now, the injured are my first priority."

"As they should be. Ah, yes," and Ongola broke off for a moment. "Joel urgently needs to know if you can estimate how much and what cargo is irretrievable?" Jim caught an indefinable note of regret in Ongola's voice that indicated he felt such a question was importunate. It was, however, totally in character for Lilienkamp and Jim was too weary to summon much rancour.

"Hell, Zi, I haven't completed a head

102

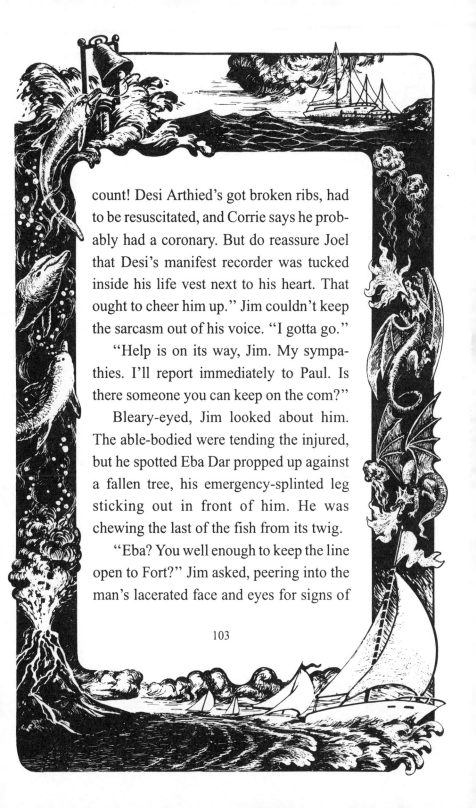

count! Desi Arthied's got broken ribs, had to be resuscitated, and Corrie says he probably had a coronary. But do reassure Joel that Desi's manifest recorder was tucked inside his life vest next to his heart. That ought to cheer him up." Jim couldn't keep the sarcasm out of his voice. "I gotta go."

"Help is on its way, Jim. My sympathies. I'll report immediately to Paul. Is there someone you can keep on the com?"

Bleary-eyed, Jim looked about him. The able-bodied were tending the injured, but he spotted Eba Dar propped up against a fallen tree, his emergency-splinted leg sticking out in front of him. He was chewing the last of the fish from its twig.

"Eba? You well enough to keep the line open to Fort?" Jim asked, peering into the man's lacerated face and eyes for signs of

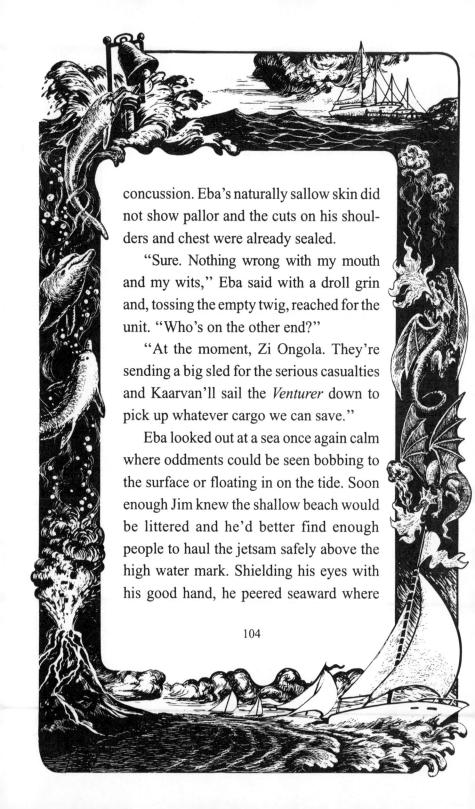

concussion. Eba's naturally sallow skin did not show pallor and the cuts on his shoulders and chest were already sealed.

"Sure. Nothing wrong with my mouth and my wits," Eba said with a droll grin and, tossing the empty twig, reached for the unit. "Who's on the other end?"

"At the moment, Zi Ongola. They're sending a big sled for the serious casualties and Kaarvan'll sail the *Venturer* down to pick up whatever cargo we can save."

Eba looked out at a sea once again calm where oddments could be seen bobbing to the surface or floating in on the tide. Soon enough Jim knew the shallow beach would be littered and he'd better find enough people to haul the jetsam safely above the high water mark. Shielding his eyes with his good hand, he peered seaward where

104

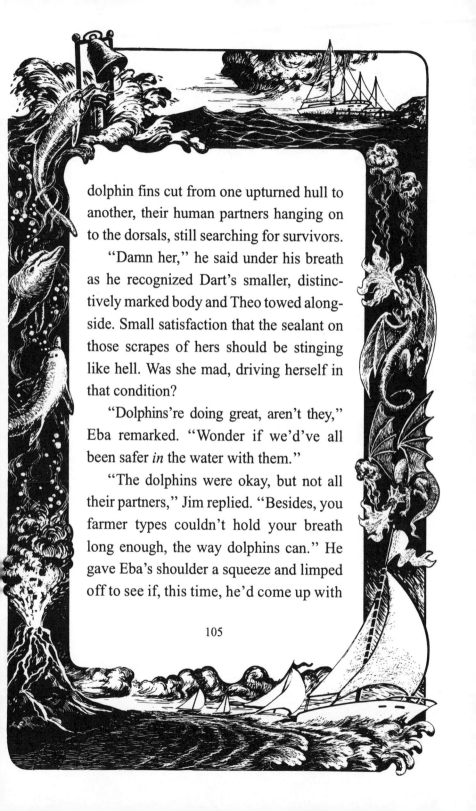

dolphin fins cut from one upturned hull to another, their human partners hanging on to the dorsals, still searching for survivors.

"Damn her," he said under his breath as he recognized Dart's smaller, distinctively marked body and Theo towed alongside. Small satisfaction that the sealant on those scrapes of hers should be stinging like hell. Was she mad, driving herself in that condition?

"Dolphins're doing great, aren't they," Eba remarked. "Wonder if we'd've all been safer *in* the water with them."

"The dolphins were okay, but not all their partners," Jim replied. "Besides, you farmer types couldn't hold your breath long enough, the way dolphins can." He gave Eba's shoulder a squeeze and limped off to see if, this time, he'd come up with

105

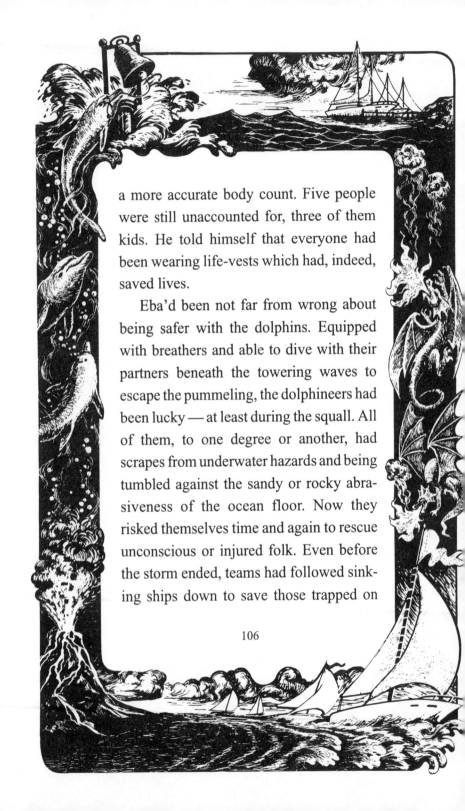

a more accurate body count. Five people were still unaccounted for, three of them kids. He told himself that everyone had been wearing life-vests which had, indeed, saved lives.

Eba'd been not far from wrong about being safer with the dolphins. Equipped with breathers and able to dive with their partners beneath the towering waves to escape the pummeling, the dolphineers had been lucky — at least during the squall. All of them, to one degree or another, had scrapes from underwater hazards and being tumbled against the sandy or rocky abra-siveness of the ocean floor. Now they risked themselves time and again to rescue unconscious or injured folk. Even before the storm ended, teams had followed sink-ing ships down to save those trapped on

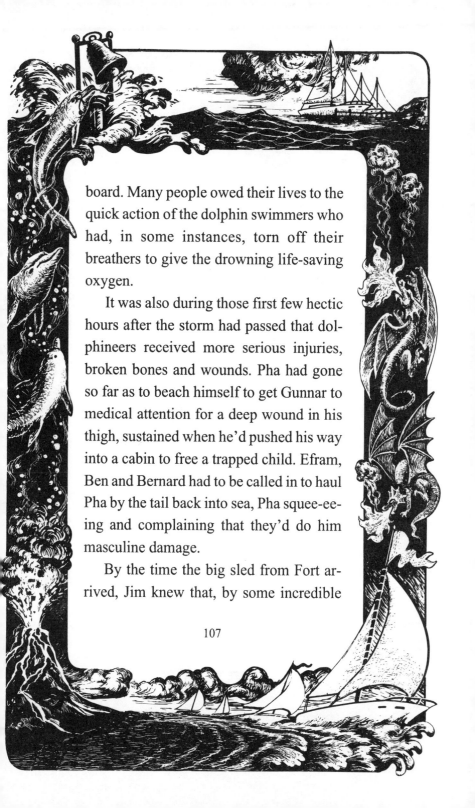

board. Many people owed their lives to the quick action of the dolphin swimmers who had, in some instances, torn off their breathers to give the drowning life-saving oxygen.

It was also during those first few hectic hours after the storm had passed that dolphineers received more serious injuries, broken bones and wounds. Pha had gone so far as to beach himself to get Gunnar to medical attention for a deep wound in his thigh, sustained when he'd pushed his way into a cabin to free a trapped child. Efram, Ben and Bernard had to be called in to haul Pha by the tail back into sea, Pha squee-ee-ing and complaining that they'd do him masculine damage.

By the time the big sled from Fort arrived, Jim knew that, by some incredible

107

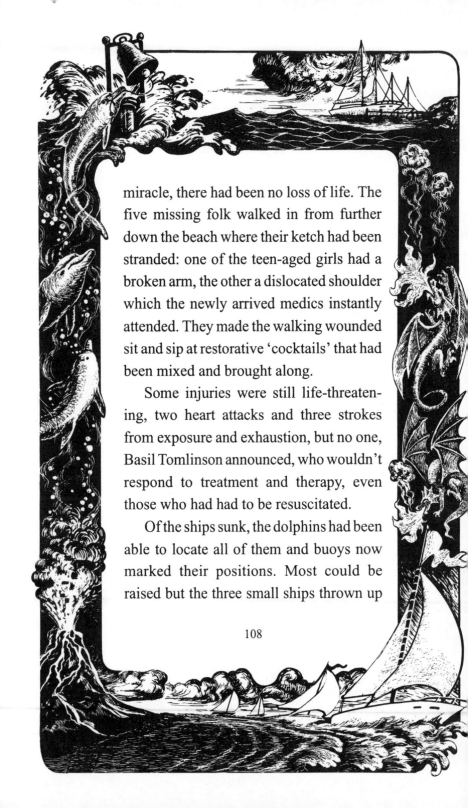

miracle, there had been no loss of life. The five missing folk walked in from further down the beach where their ketch had been stranded: one of the teen-aged girls had a broken arm, the other a dislocated shoulder which the newly arrived medics instantly attended. They made the walking wounded sit and sip at restorative 'cocktails' that had been mixed and brought along.

Some injuries were still life-threatening, two heart attacks and three strokes from exposure and exhaustion, but no one, Basil Tomlinson announced, who wouldn't respond to treatment and therapy, even those who had had to be resuscitated.

Of the ships sunk, the dolphins had been able to locate all of them and buoys now marked their positions. Most could be raised but the three small ships thrown up

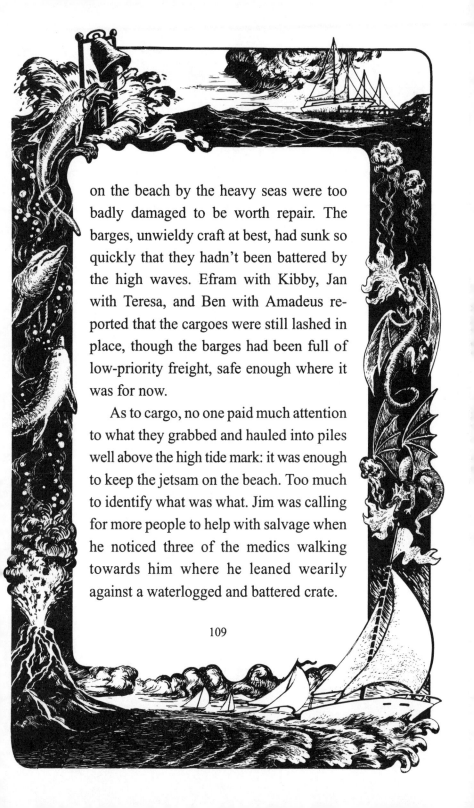

on the beach by the heavy seas were too badly damaged to be worth repair. The barges, unwieldy craft at best, had sunk so quickly that they hadn't been battered by the high waves. Efram with Kibby, Jan with Teresa, and Ben with Amadeus reported that the cargoes were still lashed in place, though the barges had been full of low-priority freight, safe enough where it was for now.

As to cargo, no one paid much attention to what they grabbed and hauled into piles well above the high tide mark: it was enough to keep the jetsam on the beach. Too much to identify what was what. Jim was calling for more people to help with salvage when he noticed three of the medics walking towards him where he leaned wearily against a waterlogged and battered crate.

109

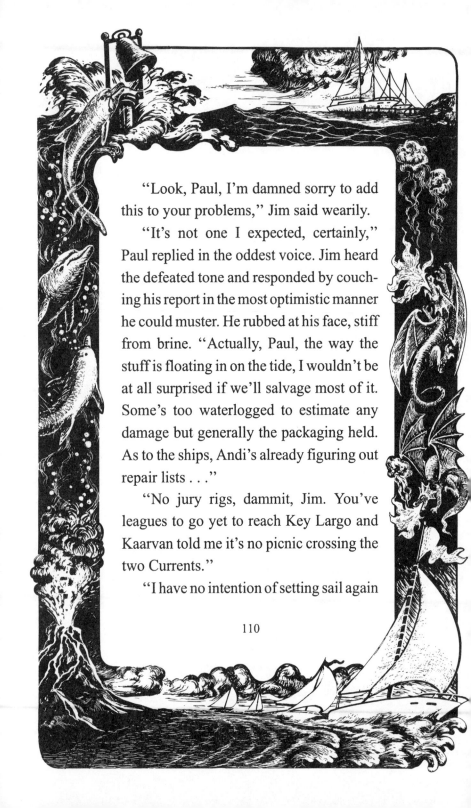

"Look, Paul, I'm damned sorry to add this to your problems," Jim said wearily.

"It's not one I expected, certainly," Paul replied in the oddest voice. Jim heard the defeated tone and responded by couching his report in the most optimistic manner he could muster. He rubbed at his face, stiff from brine. "Actually, Paul, the way the stuff is floating in on the tide, I wouldn't be at all surprised if we'll salvage most of it. Some's too waterlogged to estimate any damage but generally the packaging held. As to the ships, Andi's already figuring out repair lists . . ."

"No jury rigs, dammit, Jim. You've leagues to go yet to reach Key Largo and Kaarvan told me it's no picnic crossing the two Currents."

"I have no intention of setting sail again

110

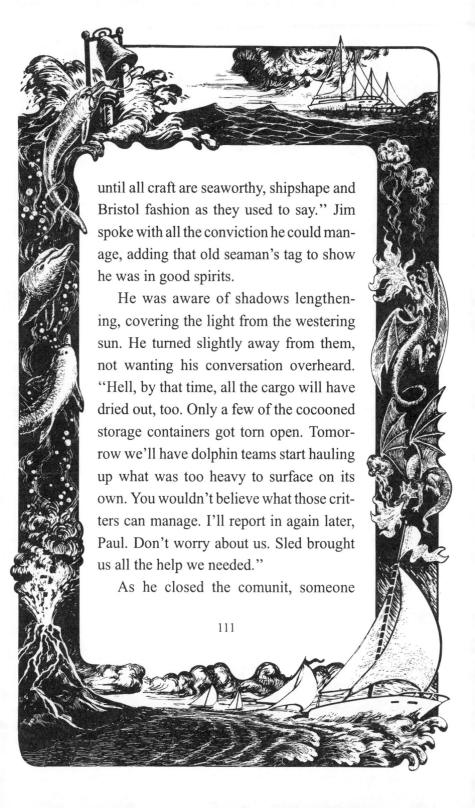

until all craft are seaworthy, shipshape and Bristol fashion as they used to say.'' Jim spoke with all the conviction he could manage, adding that old seaman's tag to show he was in good spirits.

He was aware of shadows lengthening, covering the light from the westering sun. He turned slightly away from them, not wanting his conversation overheard. ''Hell, by that time, all the cargo will have dried out, too. Only a few of the cocooned storage containers got torn open. Tomorrow we'll have dolphin teams start hauling up what was too heavy to surface on its own. You wouldn't believe what those critters can manage. I'll report in again later, Paul. Don't worry about us. Sled brought us all the help we needed.''

As he closed the comunit, someone

111

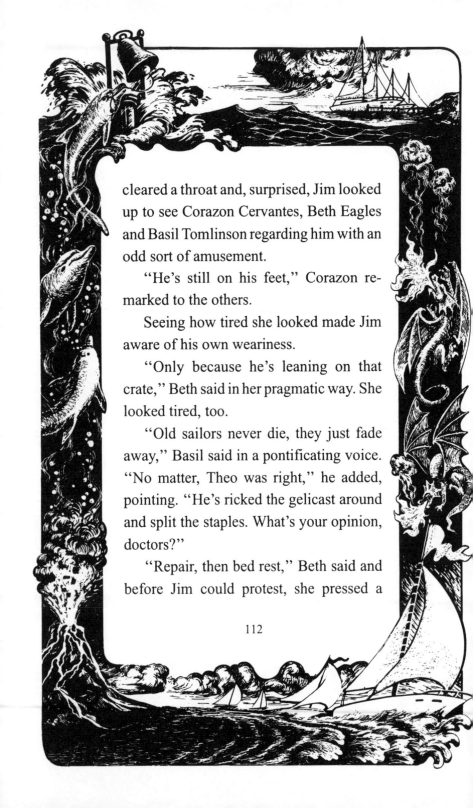

cleared a throat and, surprised, Jim looked up to see Corazon Cervantes, Beth Eagles and Basil Tomlinson regarding him with an odd sort of amusement.

"He's still on his feet," Corazon remarked to the others.

Seeing how tired she looked made Jim aware of his own weariness.

"Only because he's leaning on that crate," Beth said in her pragmatic way. She looked tired, too.

"Old sailors never die, they just fade away," Basil said in a pontificating voice. "No matter, Theo was right," he added, pointing. "He's ricked the gelicast around and split the staples. What's your opinion, doctors?"

"Repair, then bed rest," Beth said and before Jim could protest, she pressed a

112

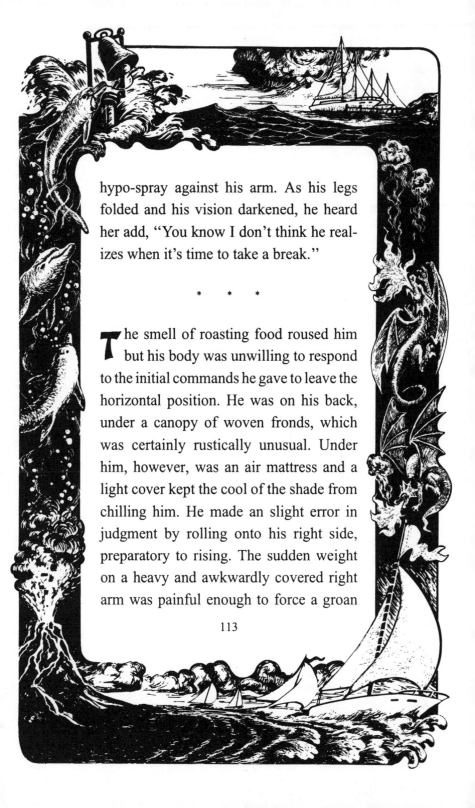

hypo-spray against his arm. As his legs folded and his vision darkened, he heard her add, "You know I don't think he realizes when it's time to take a break."

\*    \*    \*

The smell of roasting food roused him but his body was unwilling to respond to the initial commands he gave to leave the horizontal position. He was on his back, under a canopy of woven fronds, which was certainly rustically unusual. Under him, however, was an air mattress and a light cover kept the cool of the shade from chilling him. He made an slight error in judgment by rolling onto his right side, preparatory to rising. The sudden weight on a heavy and awkwardly covered right arm was painful enough to force a groan

113

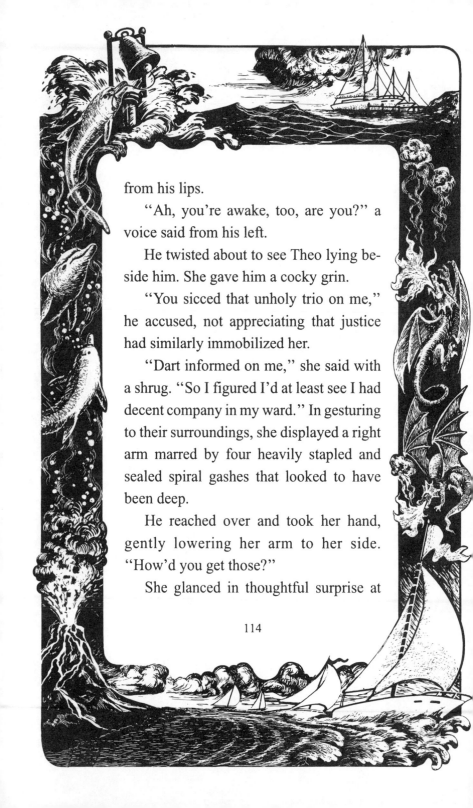

from his lips.

"Ah, you're awake, too, are you?" a voice said from his left.

He twisted about to see Theo lying beside him. She gave him a cocky grin.

"You sicced that unholy trio on me," he accused, not appreciating that justice had similarly immobilized her.

"Dart informed on me," she said with a shrug. "So I figured I'd at least see I had decent company in my ward." In gesturing to their surroundings, she displayed a right arm marred by four heavily stapled and sealed spiral gashes that looked to have been deep.

He reached over and took her hand, gently lowering her arm to her side. "How'd you get those?"

She glanced in thoughtful surprise at

114

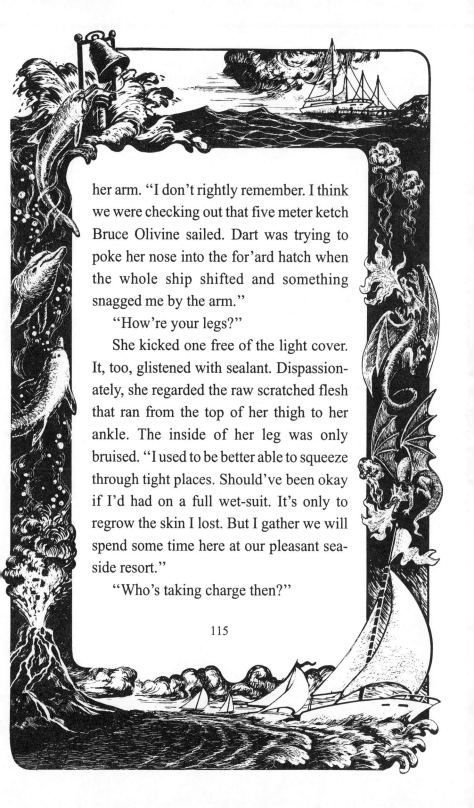

her arm. "I don't rightly remember. I think we were checking out that five meter ketch Bruce Olivine sailed. Dart was trying to poke her nose into the for'ard hatch when the whole ship shifted and something snagged me by the arm."

"How're your legs?"

She kicked one free of the light cover. It, too, glistened with sealant. Dispassionately, she regarded the raw scratched flesh that ran from the top of her thigh to her ankle. The inside of her leg was only bruised. "I used to be better able to squeeze through tight places. Should've been okay if I'd had on a full wet-suit. It's only to regrow the skin I lost. But I gather we will spend some time here at our pleasant seaside resort."

"Who's taking charge then?"

115

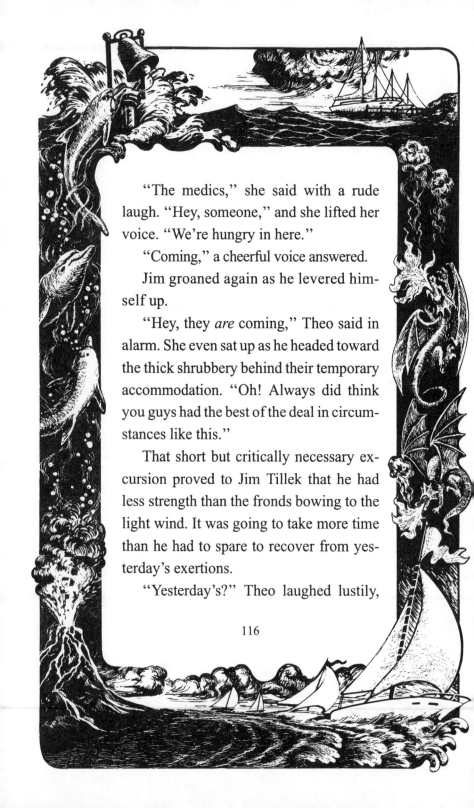

"The medics," she said with a rude laugh. "Hey, someone," and she lifted her voice. "We're hungry in here."

"Coming," a cheerful voice answered.

Jim groaned again as he levered himself up.

"Hey, they *are* coming," Theo said in alarm. She even sat up as he headed toward the thick shrubbery behind their temporary accommodation. "Oh! Always did think you guys had the best of the deal in circumstances like this."

That short but critically necessary excursion proved to Jim Tillek that he had less strength than the fronds bowing to the light wind. It was going to take more time than he had to spare to recover from yesterday's exertions.

"Yesterday's?" Theo laughed lustily,

116

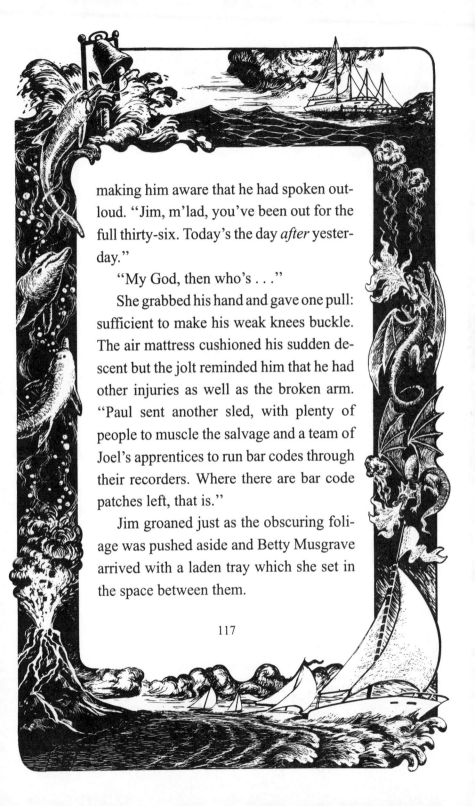

making him aware that he had spoken out-loud. "Jim, m'lad, you've been out for the full thirty-six. Today's the day *after* yester-day."

"My God, then who's . . ."

She grabbed his hand and gave one pull: sufficient to make his weak knees buckle. The air mattress cushioned his sudden de-scent but the jolt reminded him that he had other injuries as well as the broken arm. "Paul sent another sled, with plenty of people to muscle the salvage and a team of Joel's apprentices to run bar codes through their recorders. Where there are bar code patches left, that is."

Jim groaned just as the obscuring foli-age was pushed aside and Betty Musgrave arrived with a laden tray which she set in the space between them.

117

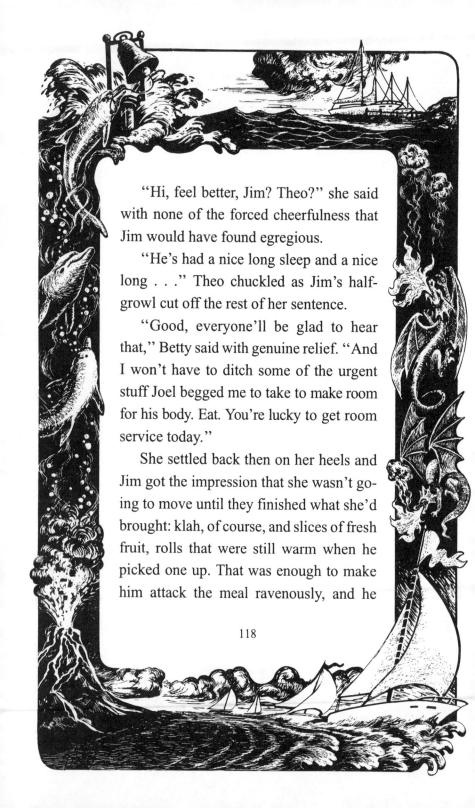

"Hi, feel better, Jim? Theo?" she said with none of the forced cheerfulness that Jim would have found egregious.

"He's had a nice long sleep and a nice long . . ." Theo chuckled as Jim's half-growl cut off the rest of her sentence.

"Good, everyone'll be glad to hear that," Betty said with genuine relief. "And I won't have to ditch some of the urgent stuff Joel begged me to take to make room for his body. Eat. You're lucky to get room service today."

She settled back then on her heels and Jim got the impression that she wasn't going to move until they finished what she'd brought: klah, of course, and slices of fresh fruit, rolls that were still warm when he picked one up. That was enough to make him attack the meal ravenously, and he

118

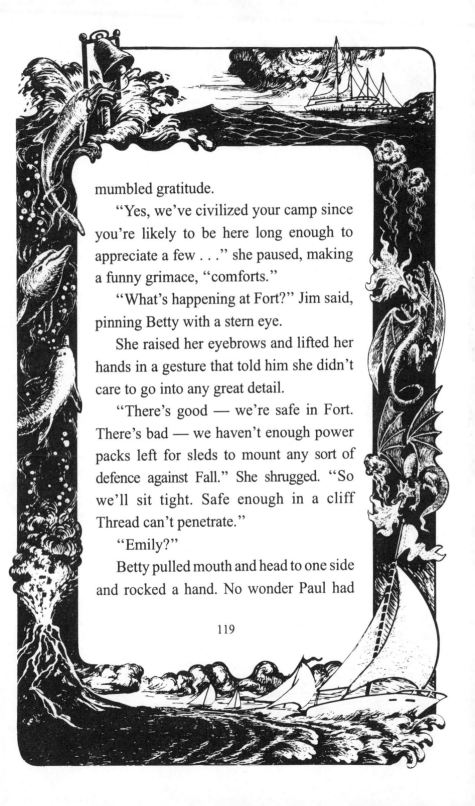

mumbled gratitude.

"Yes, we've civilized your camp since you're likely to be here long enough to appreciate a few . . ." she paused, making a funny grimace, "comforts."

"What's happening at Fort?" Jim said, pinning Betty with a stern eye.

She raised her eyebrows and lifted her hands in a gesture that told him she didn't care to go into any great detail.

"There's good — we're safe in Fort. There's bad — we haven't enough power packs left for sleds to mount any sort of defence against Fall." She shrugged. "So we'll sit tight. Safe enough in a cliff Thread can't penetrate."

"Emily?"

Betty pulled mouth and head to one side and rocked a hand. No wonder Paul had

119

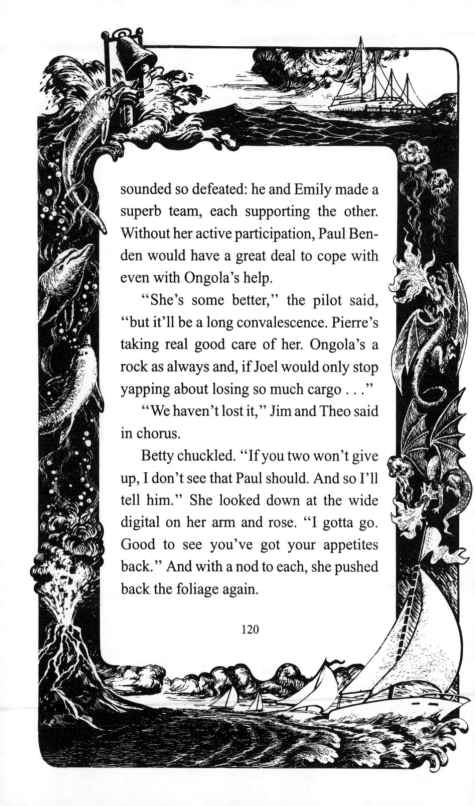

sounded so defeated: he and Emily made a superb team, each supporting the other. Without her active participation, Paul Benden would have a great deal to cope with even with Ongola's help.

"She's some better," the pilot said, "but it'll be a long convalescence. Pierre's taking real good care of her. Ongola's a rock as always and, if Joel would only stop yapping about losing so much cargo . . ."

"We haven't lost it," Jim and Theo said in chorus.

Betty chuckled. "If you two won't give up, I don't see that Paul should. And so I'll tell him." She looked down at the wide digital on her arm and rose. "I gotta go. Good to see you've got your appetites back." And with a nod to each, she pushed back the foliage again.

120

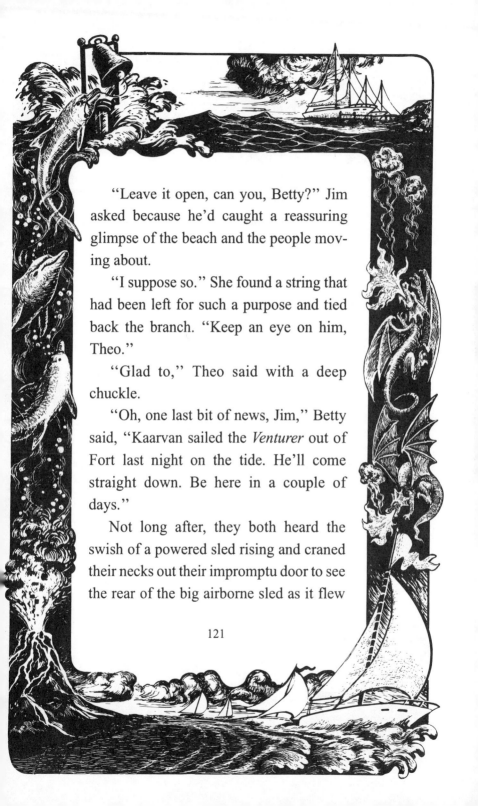

"Leave it open, can you, Betty?" Jim asked because he'd caught a reassuring glimpse of the beach and the people moving about.

"I suppose so." She found a string that had been left for such a purpose and tied back the branch. "Keep an eye on him, Theo."

"Glad to," Theo said with a deep chuckle.

"Oh, one last bit of news, Jim," Betty said, "Kaarvan sailed the *Venturer* out of Fort last night on the tide. He'll come straight down. Be here in a couple of days."

Not long after, they both heard the swish of a powered sled rising and craned their necks out their impromptu door to see the rear of the big airborne sled as it flew

121

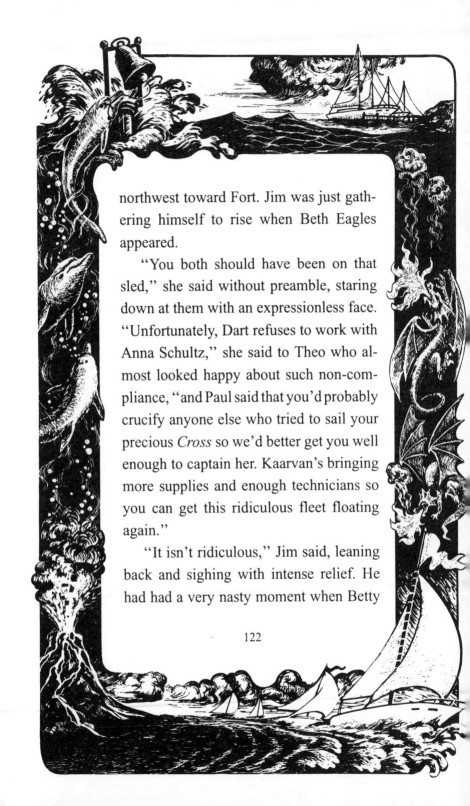

northwest toward Fort. Jim was just gath-
ering himself to rise when Beth Eagles
appeared.

"You both should have been on that
sled," she said without preamble, staring
down at them with an expressionless face.
"Unfortunately, Dart refuses to work with
Anna Schultz," she said to Theo who almost looked happy about such non-com-
pliance, "and Paul said that you'd probably
crucify anyone else who tried to sail your
precious *Cross* so we'd better get you well
enough to captain her. Kaarvan's bringing
more supplies and enough technicians so
you can get this ridiculous fleet floating
again."

"It isn't ridiculous," Jim said, leaning
back and sighing with intense relief. He
had had a very nasty moment when Betty

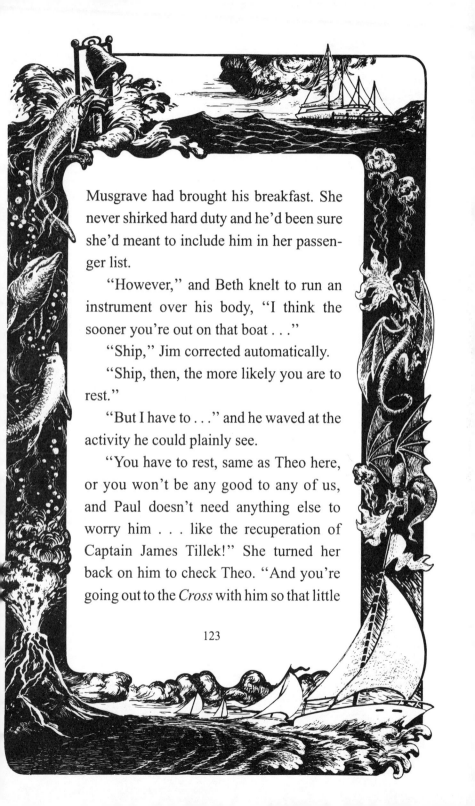

Musgrave had brought his breakfast. She never shirked hard duty and he'd been sure she'd meant to include him in her passenger list.

"However," and Beth knelt to run an instrument over his body, "I think the sooner you're out on that boat . . ."

"Ship," Jim corrected automatically.

"Ship, then, the more likely you are to rest."

"But I have to . . ." and he waved at the activity he could plainly see.

"You have to rest, same as Theo here, or you won't be any good to any of us, and Paul doesn't need anything else to worry him . . . like the recuperation of Captain James Tillek!" She turned her back on him to check Theo. "And you're going out to the *Cross* with him so that little

123

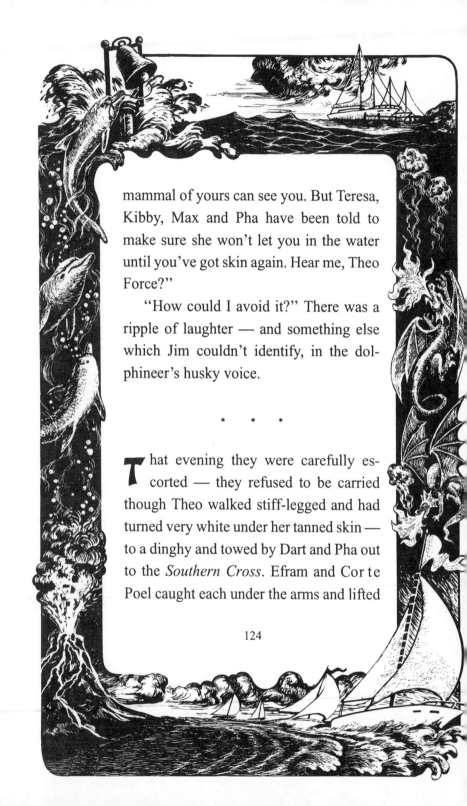

mammal of yours can see you. But Teresa, Kibby, Max and Pha have been told to make sure she won't let you in the water until you've got skin again. Hear me, Theo Force?"

"How could I avoid it?" There was a ripple of laughter — and something else which Jim couldn't identify, in the dolphineer's husky voice.

\*   \*   \*

That evening they were carefully escorted — they refused to be carried though Theo walked stiff-legged and had turned very white under her tanned skin — to a dinghy and towed by Dart and Pha out to the *Southern Cross*. Efram and Cor te Poel caught each under the arms and lifted

124

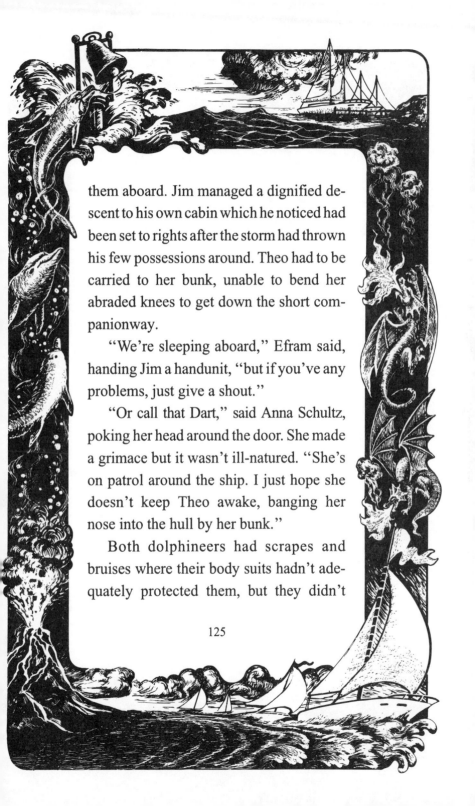

them aboard. Jim managed a dignified descent to his own cabin which he noticed had been set to rights after the storm had thrown his few possessions around. Theo had to be carried to her bunk, unable to bend her abraded knees to get down the short companionway.

"We're sleeping aboard," Efram said, handing Jim a handunit, "but if you've any problems, just give a shout."

"Or call that Dart," said Anna Schultz, poking her head around the door. She made a grimace but it wasn't ill-natured. "She's on patrol around the ship. I just hope she doesn't keep Theo awake, banging her nose into the hull by her bunk."

Both dolphineers had scrapes and bruises where their body suits hadn't adequately protected them, but they didn't

125

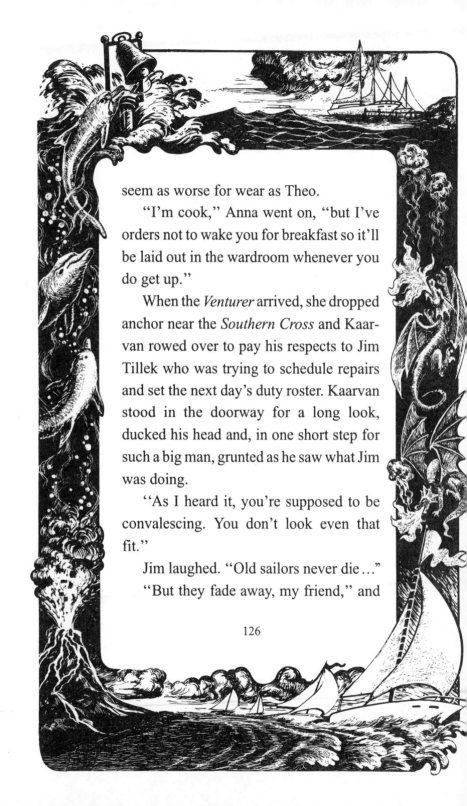

seem as worse for wear as Theo.

"I'm cook," Anna went on, "but I've orders not to wake you for breakfast so it'll be laid out in the wardroom whenever you do get up."

When the *Venturer* arrived, she dropped anchor near the *Southern Cross* and Kaarvan rowed over to pay his respects to Jim Tillek who was trying to schedule repairs and set the next day's duty roster. Kaarvan stood in the doorway for a long look, ducked his head and, in one short step for such a big man, grunted as he saw what Jim was doing.

"As I heard it, you're supposed to be convalescing. You don't look even that fit."

Jim laughed. "Old sailors never die..."

"But they fade away, my friend," and

126

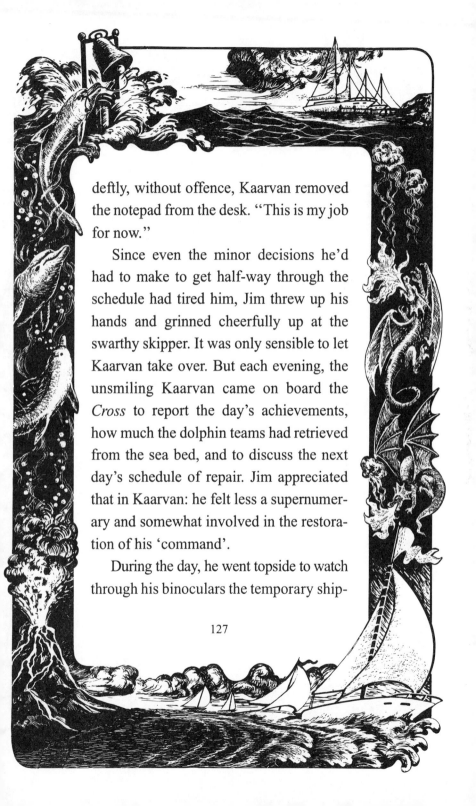

deftly, without offence, Kaarvan removed the notepad from the desk. "This is my job for now."

Since even the minor decisions he'd had to make to get half-way through the schedule had tired him, Jim threw up his hands and grinned cheerfully up at the swarthy skipper. It was only sensible to let Kaarvan take over. But each evening, the unsmiling Kaarvan came on board the *Cross* to report the day's achievements, how much the dolphin teams had retrieved from the sea bed, and to discuss the next day's schedule of repair. Jim appreciated that in Kaarvan: he felt less a supernumerary and somewhat involved in the restoration of his 'command'.

During the day, he went topside to watch through his binoculars the temporary ship-

127

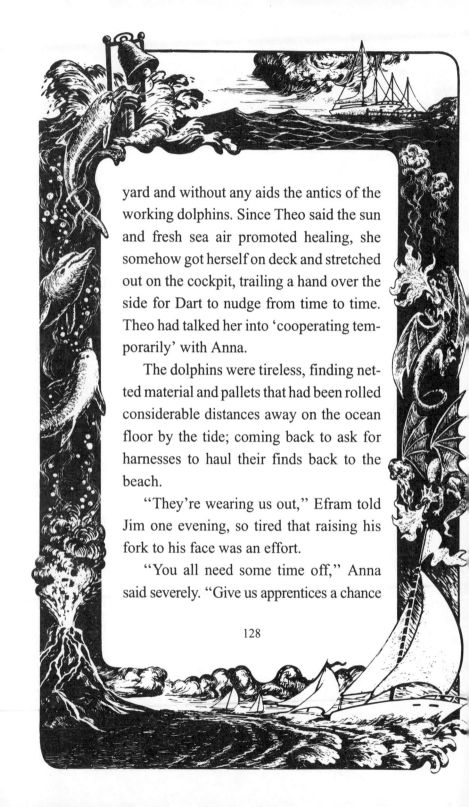

yard and without any aids the antics of the working dolphins. Since Theo said the sun and fresh sea air promoted healing, she somehow got herself on deck and stretched out on the cockpit, trailing a hand over the side for Dart to nudge from time to time. Theo had talked her into 'cooperating temporarily' with Anna.

The dolphins were tireless, finding netted material and pallets that had been rolled considerable distances away on the ocean floor by the tide; coming back to ask for harnesses to haul their finds back to the beach.

"They're wearing us out," Efram told Jim one evening, so tired that raising his fork to his face was an effort.

"You all need some time off," Anna said severely. "Give us apprentices a chance

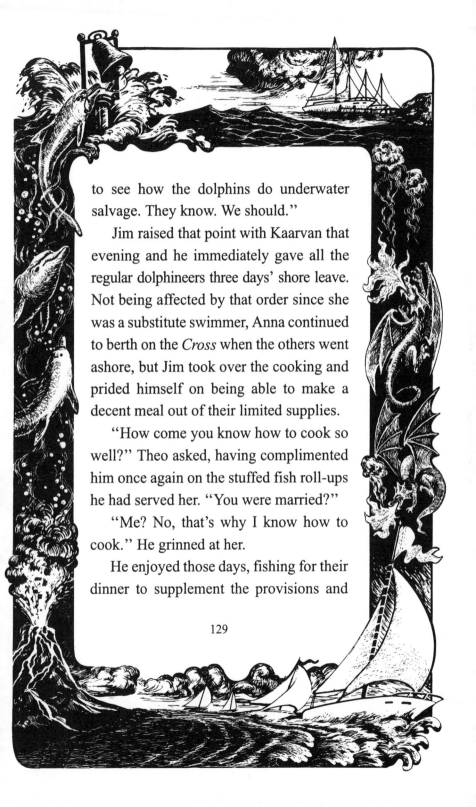

to see how the dolphins do underwater salvage. They know. We should."

Jim raised that point with Kaarvan that evening and he immediately gave all the regular dolphineers three days' shore leave. Not being affected by that order since she was a substitute swimmer, Anna continued to berth on the *Cross* when the others went ashore, but Jim took over the cooking and prided himself on being able to make a decent meal out of their limited supplies.

"How come you know how to cook so well?" Theo asked, having complimented him once again on the stuffed fish roll-ups he had served her. "You were married?"

"Me? No, that's why I know how to cook." He grinned at her.

He enjoyed those days, fishing for their dinner to supplement the provisions and

129

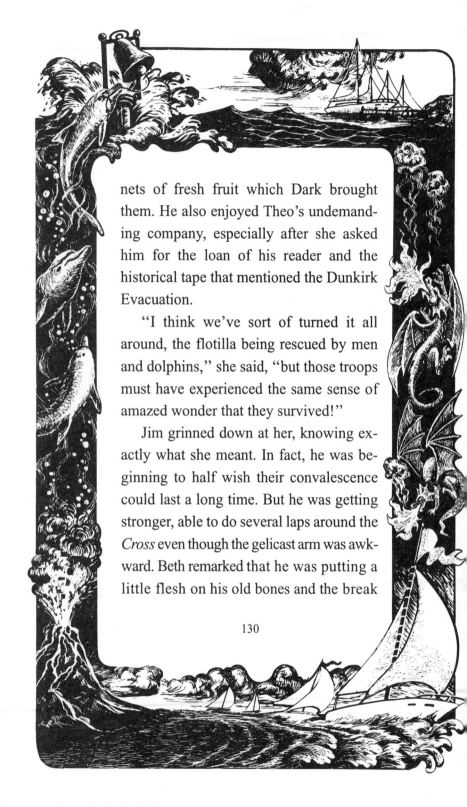

nets of fresh fruit which Dark brought them. He also enjoyed Theo's undemanding company, especially after she asked him for the loan of his reader and the historical tape that mentioned the Dunkirk Evacuation.

"I think we've sort of turned it all around, the flotilla being rescued by men and dolphins," she said, "but those troops must have experienced the same sense of amazed wonder that they survived!"

Jim grinned down at her, knowing exactly what she meant. In fact, he was beginning to half wish their convalescence could last a long time. But he was getting stronger, able to do several laps around the *Cross* even though the gelicast arm was awkward. Beth remarked that he was putting a little flesh on his old bones and the break

130

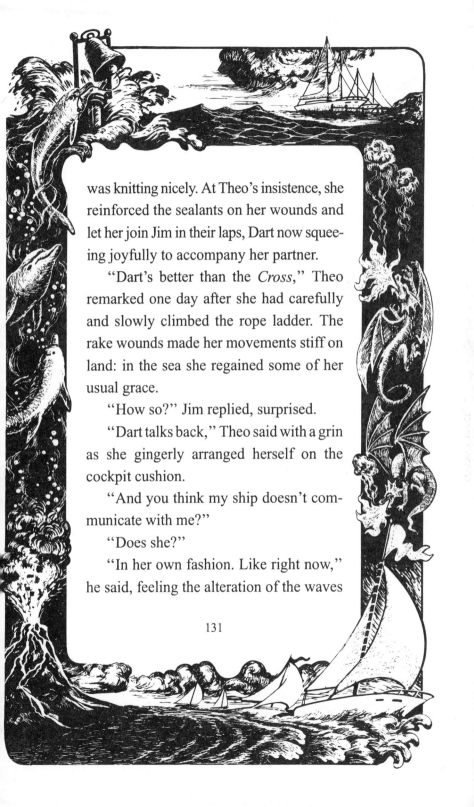

was knitting nicely. At Theo's insistence, she reinforced the sealants on her wounds and let her join Jim in their laps, Dart now squeeing joyfully to accompany her partner.

"Dart's better than the *Cross*," Theo remarked one day after she had carefully and slowly climbed the rope ladder. The rake wounds made her movements stiff on land: in the sea she regained some of her usual grace.

"How so?" Jim replied, surprised.

"Dart talks back," Theo said with a grin as she gingerly arranged herself on the cockpit cushion.

"And you think my ship doesn't communicate with me?"

"Does she?"

"In her own fashion. Like right now," he said, feeling the alteration of the waves

131

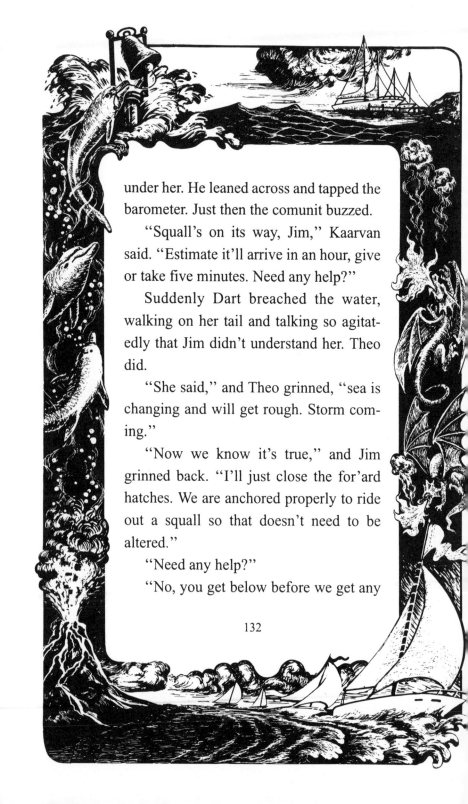

under her. He leaned across and tapped the barometer. Just then the comunit buzzed.

"Squall's on its way, Jim," Kaarvan said. "Estimate it'll arrive in an hour, give or take five minutes. Need any help?"

Suddenly Dart breached the water, walking on her tail and talking so agitatedly that Jim didn't understand her. Theo did.

"She said," and Theo grinned, "sea is changing and will get rough. Storm coming."

"Now we know it's true," and Jim grinned back. "I'll just close the for'ard hatches. We are anchored properly to ride out a squall so that doesn't need to be altered."

"Need any help?"

"No, you get below before we get any

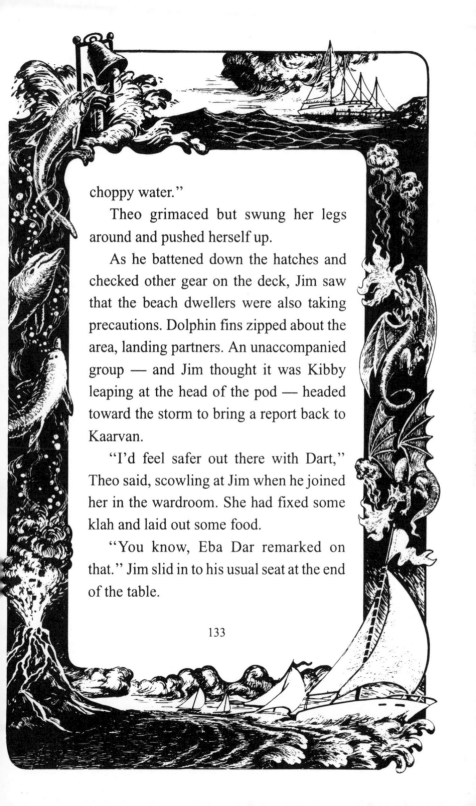

choppy water."

Theo grimaced but swung her legs around and pushed herself up.

As he battened down the hatches and checked other gear on the deck, Jim saw that the beach dwellers were also taking precautions. Dolphin fins zipped about the area, landing partners. An unaccompanied group — and Jim thought it was Kibby leaping at the head of the pod — headed toward the storm to bring a report back to Kaarvan.

"I'd feel safer out there with Dart," Theo said, scowling at Jim when he joined her in the wardroom. She had fixed some klah and laid out some food.

"You know, Eba Dar remarked on that." Jim slid in to his usual seat at the end of the table.

133

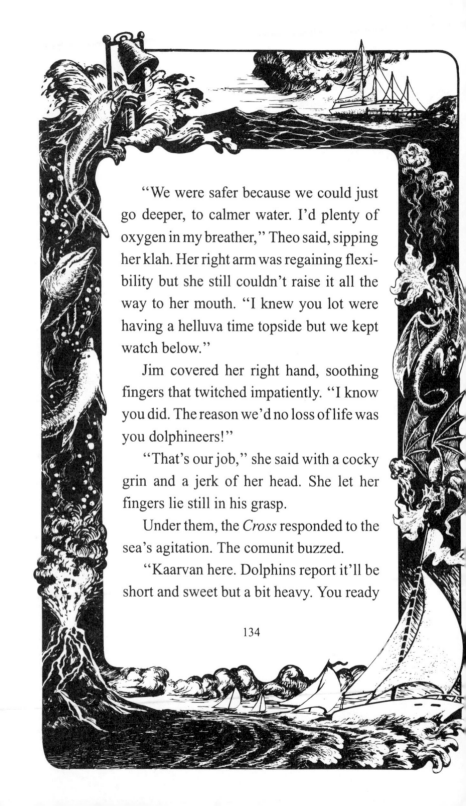

"We were safer because we could just go deeper, to calmer water. I'd plenty of oxygen in my breather," Theo said, sipping her klah. Her right arm was regaining flexibility but she still couldn't raise it all the way to her mouth. "I knew you lot were having a helluva time topside but we kept watch below."

Jim covered her right hand, soothing fingers that twitched impatiently. "I know you did. The reason we'd no loss of life was you dolphineers!"

"That's our job," she said with a cocky grin and a jerk of her head. She let her fingers lie still in his grasp.

Under them, the *Cross* responded to the sea's agitation. The comunit buzzed.

"Kaarvan here. Dolphins report it'll be short and sweet but a bit heavy. You ready

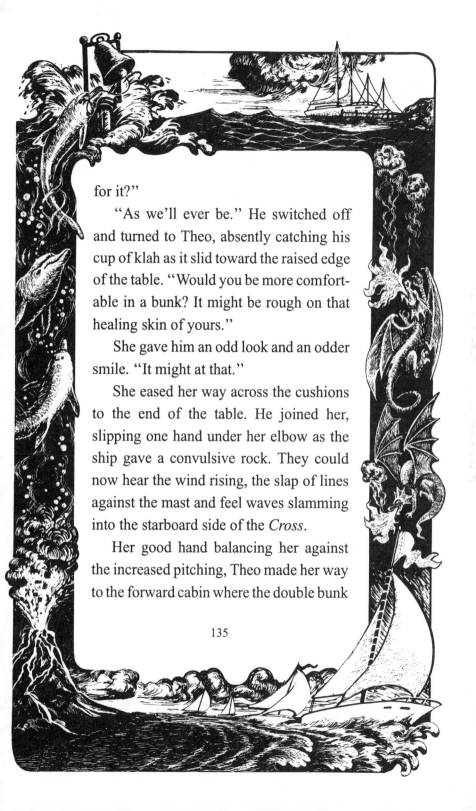

for it?"

"As we'll ever be." He switched off and turned to Theo, absently catching his cup of klah as it slid toward the raised edge of the table. "Would you be more comfortable in a bunk? It might be rough on that healing skin of yours."

She gave him an odd look and an odder smile. "It might at that."

She eased her way across the cushions to the end of the table. He joined her, slipping one hand under her elbow as the ship gave a convulsive rock. They could now hear the wind rising, the slap of lines against the mast and feel waves slamming into the starboard side of the *Cross*.

Her good hand balancing her against the increased pitching, Theo made her way to the forward cabin where the double bunk

135

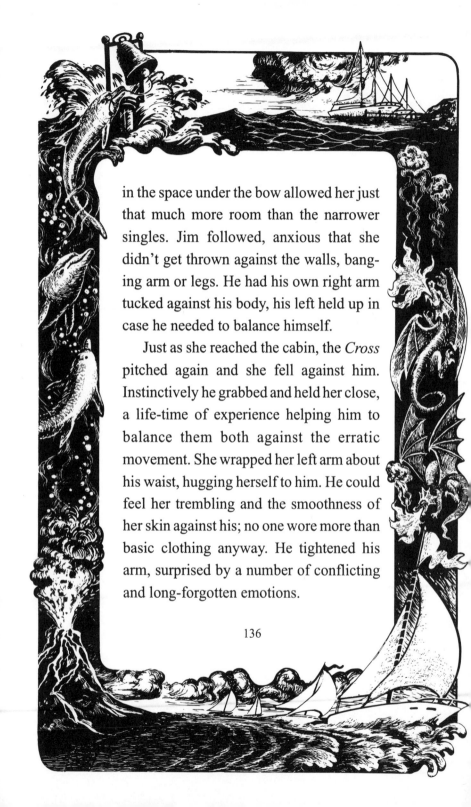

in the space under the bow allowed her just
that much more room than the narrower
singles. Jim followed, anxious that she
didn't get thrown against the walls, banging arm or legs. He had his own right arm
tucked against his body, his left held up in
case he needed to balance himself.

Just as she reached the cabin, the *Cross*
pitched again and she fell against him.
Instinctively he grabbed and held her close,
a life-time of experience helping him to
balance them both against the erratic
movement. She wrapped her left arm about
his waist, hugging herself to him. He could
feel her trembling and the smoothness of
her skin against his; no one wore more than
basic clothing anyway. He tightened his
arm, surprised by a number of conflicting
and long-forgotten emotions.

136

"It won't be as bad a blow as the other one," he said, thinking to reassure her. Though why Theo would need reassurance . . .

"I'm not scared, you iggerant old fool," she said in a taut voice. Switching her left arm to around his neck, she hauled his head down to hers and kissed him so thoroughly that he lost his balance and they both tumbled into the cabin as the *Cross* took part in this matter and pitched them forward. Nor would Theo let go of him even after they had fallen across one of the smaller bunks.

"Your legs? Your arm," Jim began without lessening the pressure his right arm exerted in keeping them together. "I'll hurt you . . ."

"There are ways, dammit, Jim Tillek, there are ways!"

137

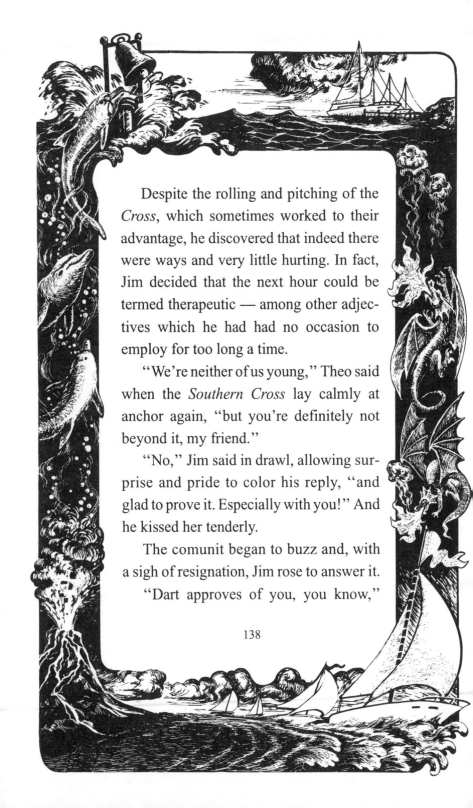

Despite the rolling and pitching of the *Cross*, which sometimes worked to their advantage, he discovered that indeed there were ways and very little hurting. In fact, Jim decided that the next hour could be termed therapeutic — among other adjectives which he had had no occasion to employ for too long a time.

"We're neither of us young," Theo said when the *Southern Cross* lay calmly at anchor again, "but you're definitely not beyond it, my friend."

"No," Jim said in drawl, allowing surprise and pride to color his reply, "and glad to prove it. Especially with you!" And he kissed her tenderly.

The comunit began to buzz and, with a sigh of resignation, Jim rose to answer it.

"Dart approves of you, you know,"

138

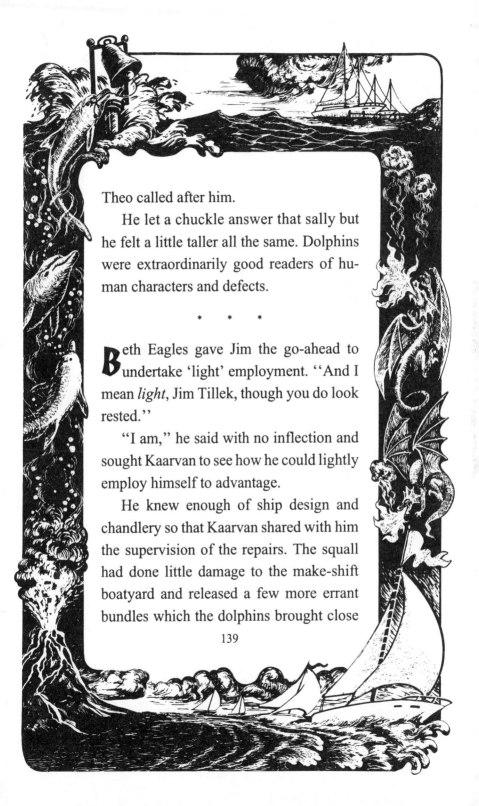

Theo called after him.

He let a chuckle answer that sally but he felt a little taller all the same. Dolphins were extraordinarily good readers of human characters and defects.

*   *   *

Beth Eagles gave Jim the go-ahead to undertake 'light' employment. ''And I mean *light*, Jim Tillek, though you do look rested.''

"I am," he said with no inflection and sought Kaarvan to see how he could lightly employ himself to advantage.

He knew enough of ship design and chandlery so that Kaarvan shared with him the supervision of the repairs. The squall had done little damage to the make-shift boatyard and released a few more errant bundles which the dolphins brought close

139

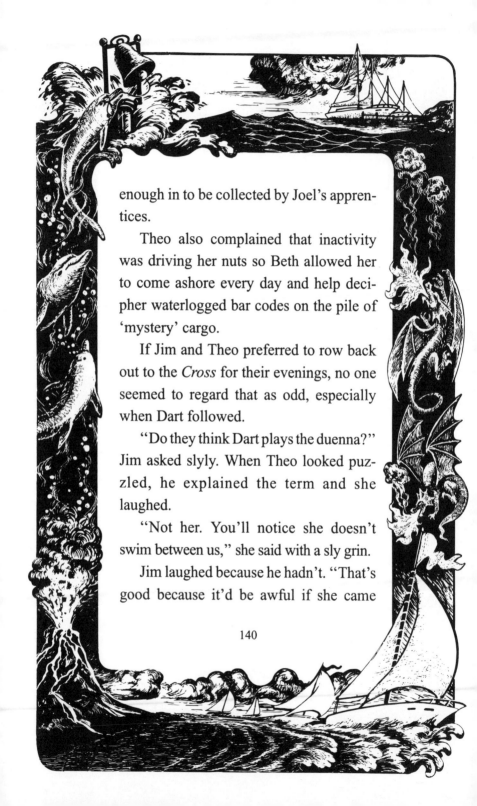

enough in to be collected by Joel's apprentices.

Theo also complained that inactivity was driving her nuts so Beth allowed her to come ashore every day and help decipher waterlogged bar codes on the pile of 'mystery' cargo.

If Jim and Theo preferred to row back out to the *Cross* for their evenings, no one seemed to regard that as odd, especially when Dart followed.

"Do they think Dart plays the duenna?" Jim asked slyly. When Theo looked puzzled, he explained the term and she laughed.

"Not her. You'll notice she doesn't swim between us," she said with a sly grin.

Jim laughed because he hadn't. "That's good because it'd be awful if she came

140

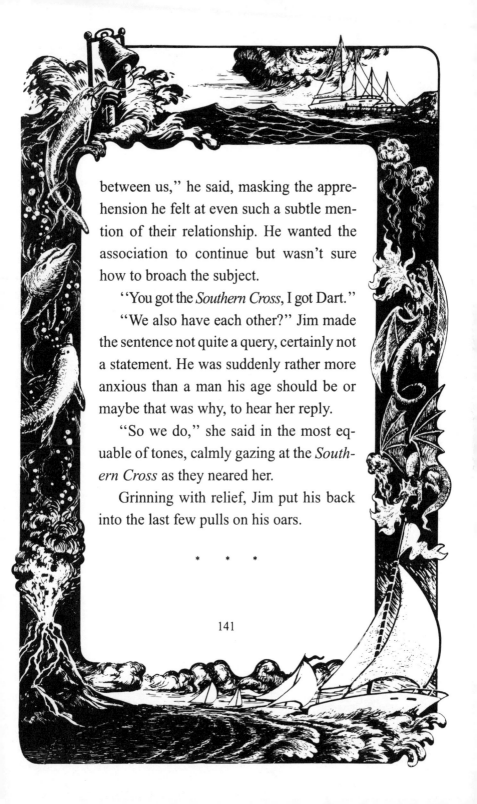

between us," he said, masking the apprehension he felt at even such a subtle mention of their relationship. He wanted the association to continue but wasn't sure how to broach the subject.

"You got the *Southern Cross*, I got Dart."

"We also have each other?" Jim made the sentence not quite a query, certainly not a statement. He was suddenly rather more anxious than a man his age should be or maybe that was why, to hear her reply.

"So we do," she said in the most equable of tones, calmly gazing at the *Southern Cross* as they neared her.

Grinning with relief, Jim put his back into the last few pulls on his oars.

\*   \*   \*

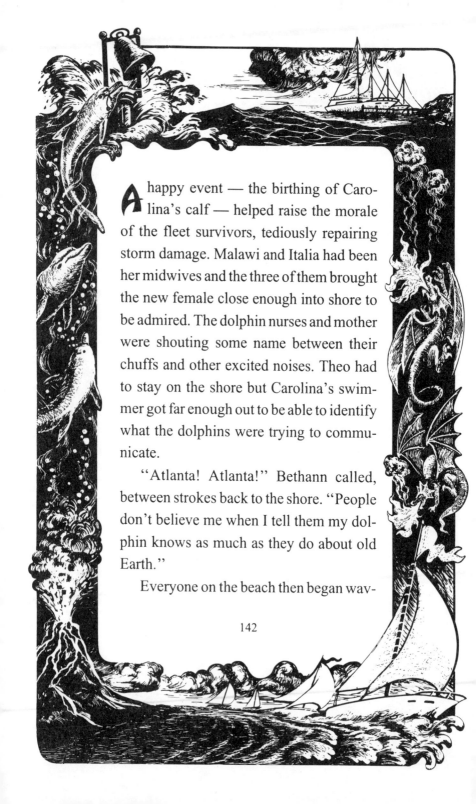

A happy event — the birthing of Carolina's calf — helped raise the morale of the fleet survivors, tediously repairing storm damage. Malawi and Italia had been her midwives and the three of them brought the new female close enough into shore to be admired. The dolphin nurses and mother were shouting some name between their chuffs and other excited noises. Theo had to stay on the shore but Carolina's swimmer got far enough out to be able to identify what the dolphins were trying to communicate.

"Atlanta! Atlanta!" Bethann called, between strokes back to the shore. "People don't believe me when I tell them my dolphin knows as much as they do about old Earth."

Everyone on the beach then began wav-

142

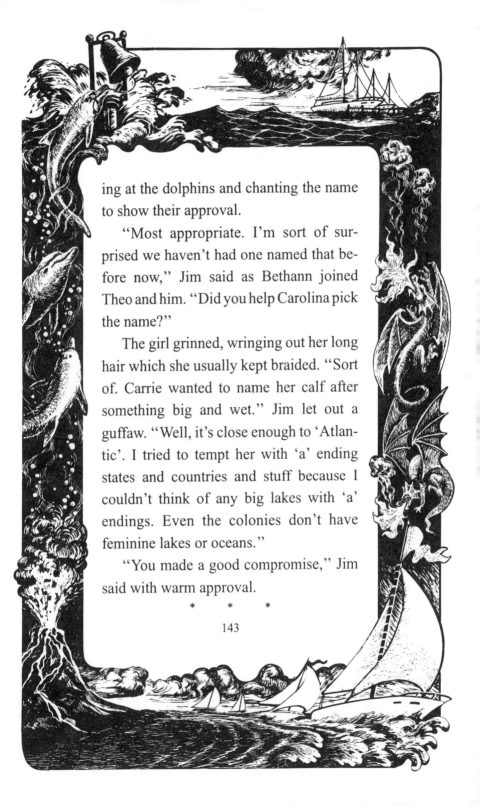

ing at the dolphins and chanting the name to show their approval.

"Most appropriate. I'm sort of surprised we haven't had one named that before now," Jim said as Bethann joined Theo and him. "Did you help Carolina pick the name?"

The girl grinned, wringing out her long hair which she usually kept braided. "Sort of. Carrie wanted to name her calf after something big and wet." Jim let out a guffaw. "Well, it's close enough to 'Atlantic'. I tried to tempt her with 'a' ending states and countries and stuff because I couldn't think of any big lakes with 'a' endings. Even the colonies don't have feminine lakes or oceans."

"You made a good compromise," Jim said with warm approval.

\*　　\*　　\*

143

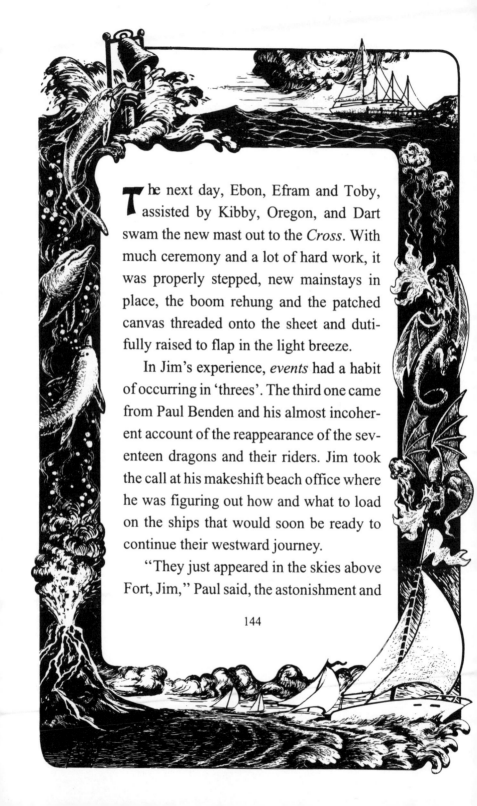

The next day, Ebon, Efram and Toby, assisted by Kibby, Oregon, and Dart swam the new mast out to the *Cross*. With much ceremony and a lot of hard work, it was properly stepped, new mainstays in place, the boom rehung and the patched canvas threaded onto the sheet and dutifully raised to flap in the light breeze.

In Jim's experience, *events* had a habit of occurring in 'threes'. The third one came from Paul Benden and his almost incoherent account of the reappearance of the seventeen dragons and their riders. Jim took the call at his makeshift beach office where he was figuring out how and what to load on the ships that would soon be ready to continue their westward journey.

"They just appeared in the skies above Fort, Jim," Paul said, the astonishment and

144

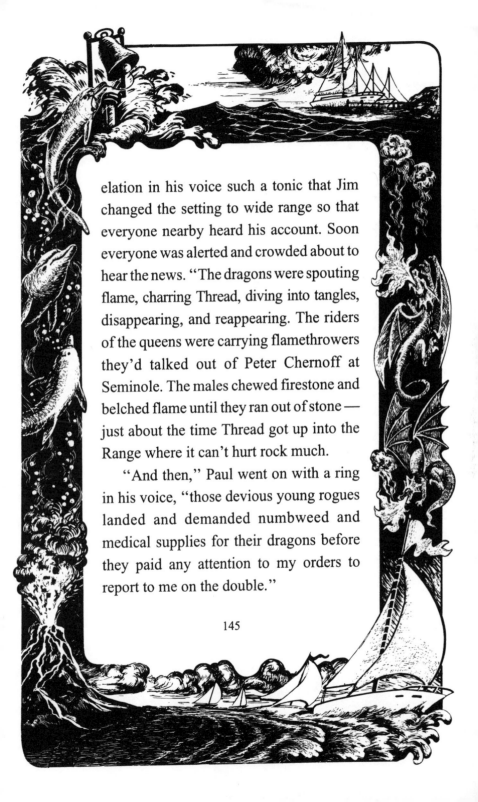

elation in his voice such a tonic that Jim
changed the setting to wide range so that
everyone nearby heard his account. Soon
everyone was alerted and crowded about to
hear the news. "The dragons were spouting
flame, charring Thread, diving into tangles,
disappearing, and reappearing. The riders
of the queens were carrying flamethrowers
they'd talked out of Peter Chernoff at
Seminole. The males chewed firestone and
belched flame until they ran out of stone —
just about the time Thread got up into the
Range where it can't hurt rock much.

"And then," Paul went on with a ring
in his voice, "those devious young rogues
landed and demanded numbweed and
medical supplies for their dragons before
they paid any attention to my orders to
report to me on the double."

145

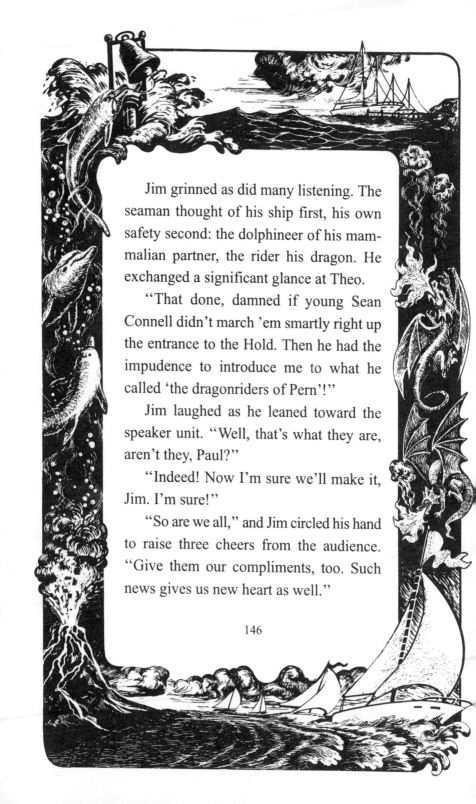

Jim grinned as did many listening. The seaman thought of his ship first, his own safety second: the dolphineer of his mammalian partner, the rider his dragon. He exchanged a significant glance at Theo.

"That done, damned if young Sean Connell didn't march 'em smartly right up the entrance to the Hold. Then he had the impudence to introduce me to what he called 'the dragonriders of Pern'!"

Jim laughed as he leaned toward the speaker unit. "Well, that's what they are, aren't they, Paul?"

"Indeed! Now I'm sure we'll make it, Jim. I'm sure!"

"So are we all," and Jim circled his hand to raise three cheers from the audience. "Give them our compliments, too. Such news gives us new heart as well."

146

He was surprised to see Theo wiping tears from her eyes and, later, when they lay beside each other in the double bunk, asked her why.

"Look, swimming with Dart is the best thing — well, almost the best thing," and she grinned at him, "that ever happened to me. But I think flying a fighting dragon would be a notch . . . well, maybe several notches above that, given the fact they're our equivalent of the battle of Dunkirk. So few against so much."

\*   \*   \*

All the work seemed to finish up at the same time which Kaarvan said was the result of good planning and Jim was equally certain was due to the boost in morale. So they loaded the *Pernese Ven-*

147

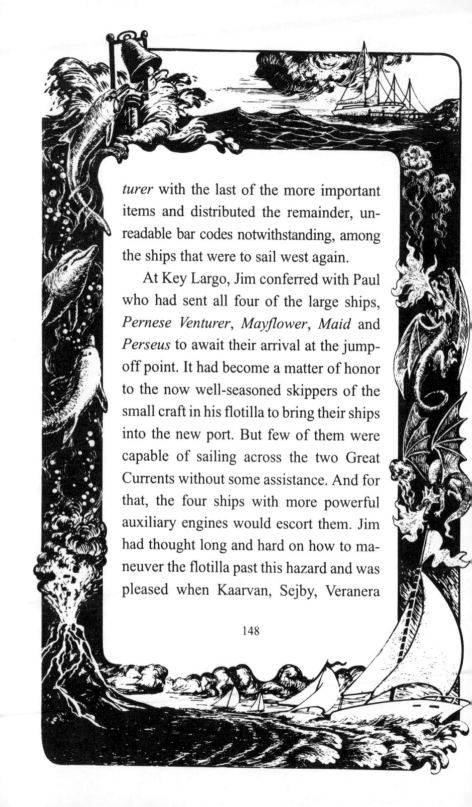

*turer* with the last of the more important items and distributed the remainder, unreadable bar codes notwithstanding, among the ships that were to sail west again.

At Key Largo, Jim conferred with Paul who had sent all four of the large ships, *Pernese Venturer*, *Mayflower*, *Maid* and *Perseus* to await their arrival at the jump-off point. It had become a matter of honor to the now well-seasoned skippers of the small craft in his flotilla to bring their ships into the new port. But few of them were capable of sailing across the two Great Currents without some assistance. And for that, the four ships with more powerful auxiliary engines would escort them. Jim had thought long and hard on how to maneuver the flotilla past this hazard and was pleased when Kaarvan, Sejby, Veranera

148

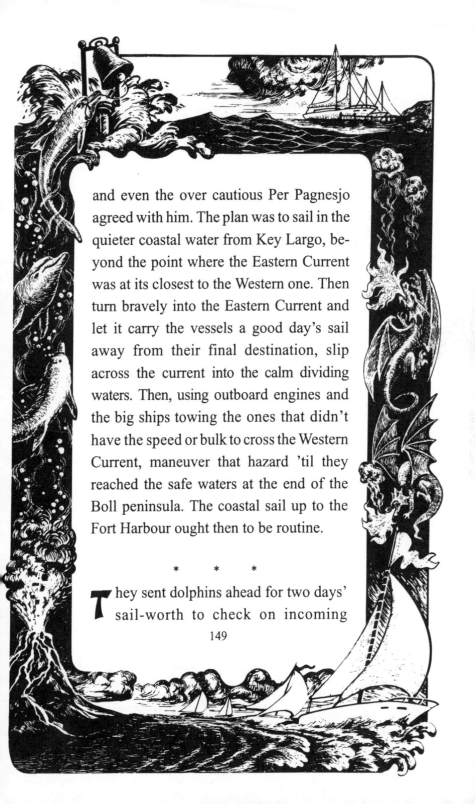

and even the over cautious Per Pagnesjo agreed with him. The plan was to sail in the quieter coastal water from Key Largo, beyond the point where the Eastern Current was at its closest to the Western one. Then turn bravely into the Eastern Current and let it carry the vessels a good day's sail away from their final destination, slip across the current into the calm dividing waters. Then, using outboard engines and the big ships towing the ones that didn't have the speed or bulk to cross the Western Current, maneuver that hazard 'til they reached the safe waters at the end of the Boll peninsula. The coastal sail up to the Fort Harbour ought then to be routine.

\*     \*     \*

They sent dolphins ahead for two days' sail-worth to check on incoming

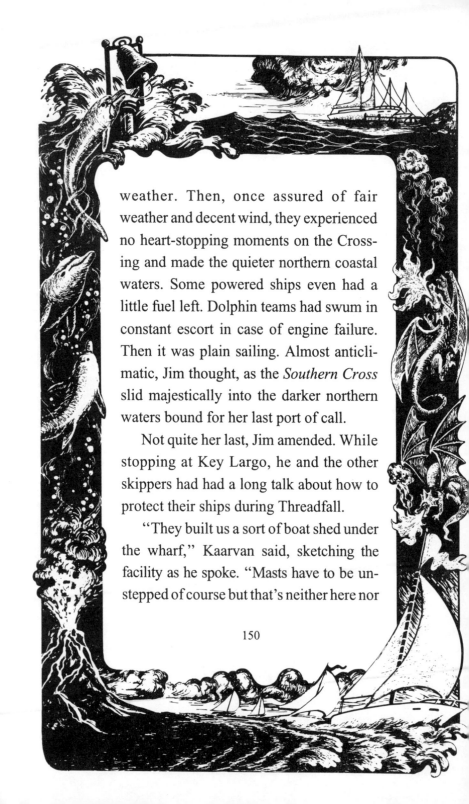

weather. Then, once assured of fair weather and decent wind, they experienced no heart-stopping moments on the Crossing and made the quieter northern coastal waters. Some powered ships even had a little fuel left. Dolphin teams had swum in constant escort in case of engine failure. Then it was plain sailing. Almost anticlimatic, Jim thought, as the *Southern Cross* slid majestically into the darker northern waters bound for her last port of call.

Not quite her last, Jim amended. While stopping at Key Largo, he and the other skippers had had a long talk about how to protect their ships during Threadfall.

"They built us a sort of boat shed under the wharf," Kaarvan said, sketching the facility as he spoke. "Masts have to be unstepped of course but that's neither here nor

150

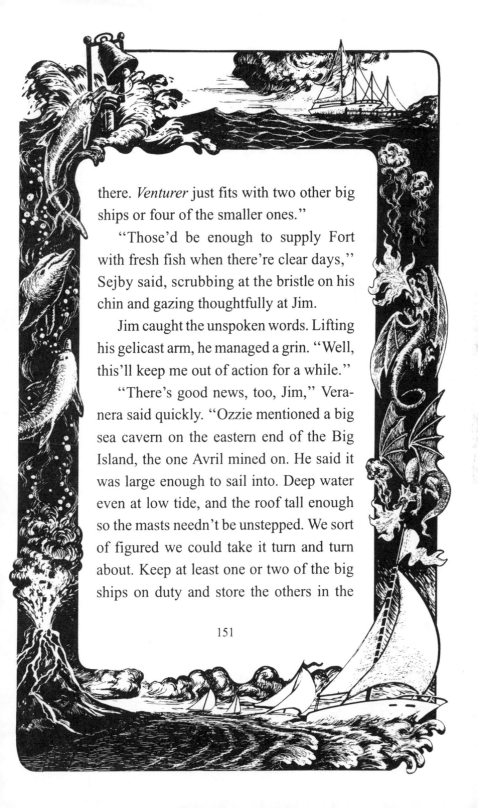

there. *Venturer* just fits with two other big ships or four of the smaller ones."

"Those'd be enough to supply Fort with fresh fish when there're clear days," Sejby said, scrubbing at the bristle on his chin and gazing thoughtfully at Jim.

Jim caught the unspoken words. Lifting his gelicast arm, he managed a grin. "Well, this'll keep me out of action for a while."

"There's good news, too, Jim," Veranera said quickly. "Ozzie mentioned a big sea cavern on the eastern end of the Big Island, the one Avril mined on. He said it was large enough to sail into. Deep water even at low tide, and the roof tall enough so the masts needn't be unstepped. We sort of figured we could take it turn and turn about. Keep at least one or two of the big ships on duty and store the others in the

151

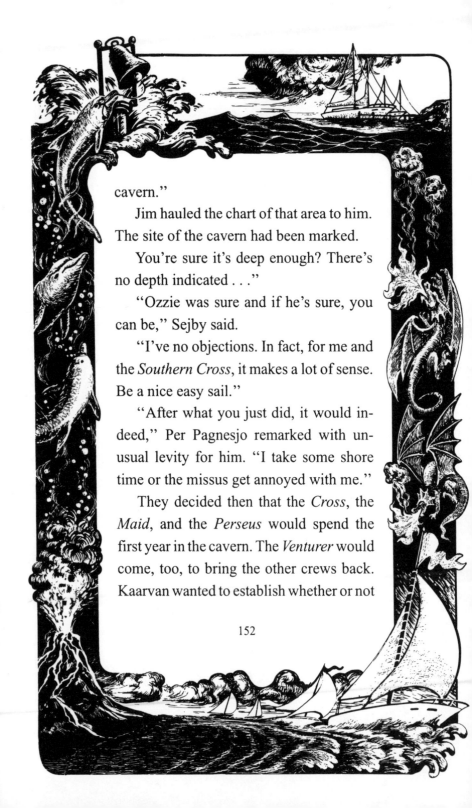

cavern."

Jim hauled the chart of that area to him. The site of the cavern had been marked.

You're sure it's deep enough? There's no depth indicated . . ."

"Ozzie was sure and if he's sure, you can be," Sejby said.

"I've no objections. In fact, for me and the *Southern Cross*, it makes a lot of sense. Be a nice easy sail."

"After what you just did, it would indeed," Per Pagnesjo remarked with unusual levity for him. "I take some shore time or the missus get annoyed with me."

They decided then that the *Cross*, the *Maid*, and the *Perseus* would spend the first year in the cavern. The *Venturer* would come, too, to bring the other crews back. Kaarvan wanted to establish whether or not

152

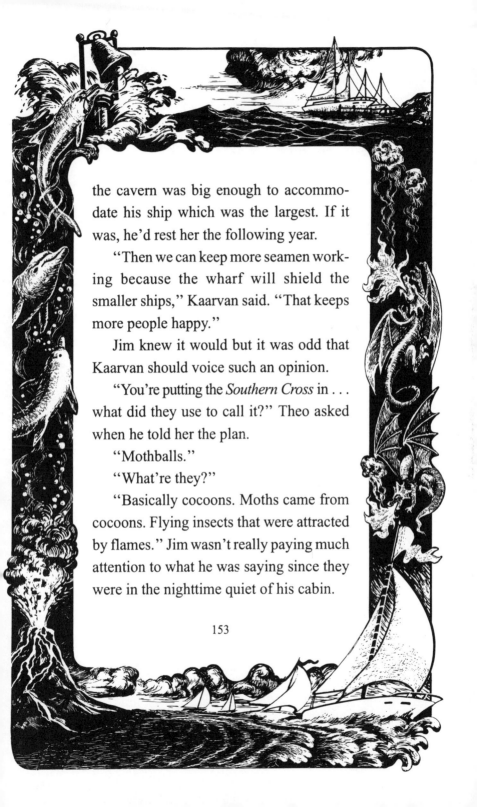

the cavern was big enough to accommo-
date his ship which was the largest. If it
was, he'd rest her the following year.

"Then we can keep more seamen working because the wharf will shield the
smaller ships," Kaarvan said. "That keeps
more people happy."

Jim knew it would but it was odd that
Kaarvan should voice such an opinion.

"You're putting the *Southern Cross* in . . .
what did they use to call it?" Theo asked
when he told her the plan.

"Mothballs."

"What're they?"

"Basically cocoons. Moths came from
cocoons. Flying insects that were attracted
by flames." Jim wasn't really paying much
attention to what he was saying since they
were in the nighttime quiet of his cabin.

153

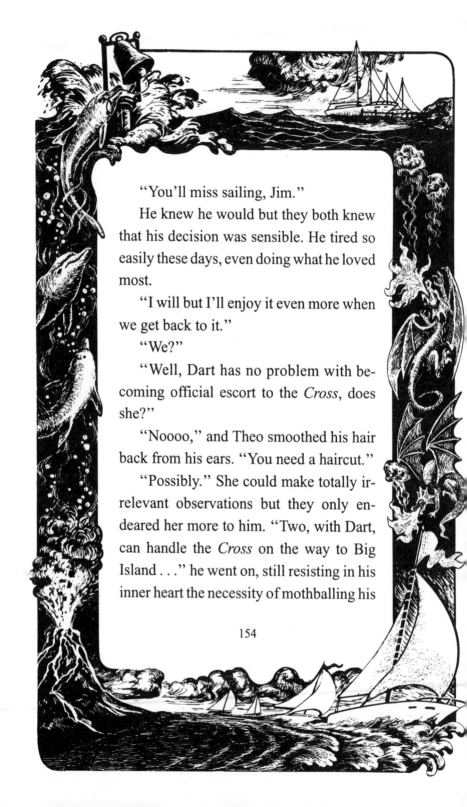

"You'll miss sailing, Jim."

He knew he would but they both knew that his decision was sensible. He tired so easily these days, even doing what he loved most.

"I will but I'll enjoy it even more when we get back to it."

"We?"

"Well, Dart has no problem with becoming official escort to the *Cross*, does she?"

"Noooo," and Theo smoothed his hair back from his ears. "You need a haircut."

"Possibly." She could make totally irrelevant observations but they only endeared her more to him. "Two, with Dart, can handle the *Cross* on the way to Big Island . . ." he went on, still resisting in his inner heart the necessity of mothballing his

154

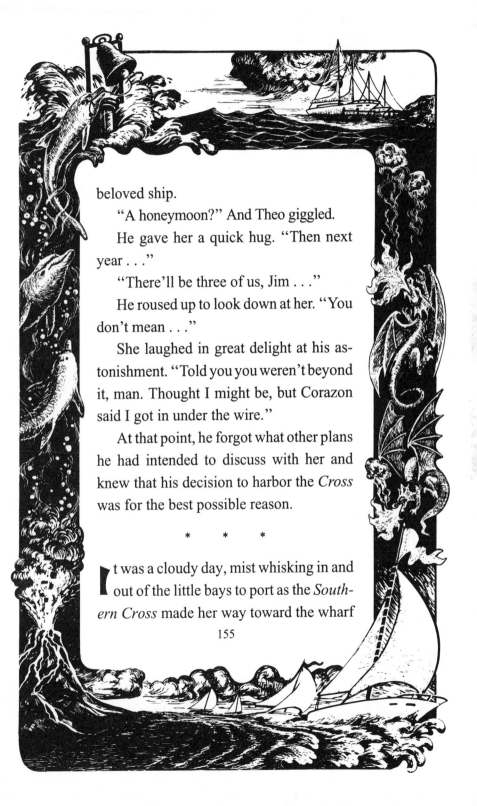

beloved ship.

"A honeymoon?" And Theo giggled.

He gave her a quick hug. "Then next year . . ."

"There'll be three of us, Jim . . ."

He roused up to look down at her. "You don't mean . . ."

She laughed in great delight at his astonishment. "Told you you weren't beyond it, man. Thought I might be, but Corazon said I got in under the wire."

At that point, he forgot what other plans he had intended to discuss with her and knew that his decision to harbor the *Cross* was for the best possible reason.

\*　　\*　　\*

It was a cloudy day, mist whisking in and out of the little bays to port as the *Southern Cross* made her way toward the wharf

155

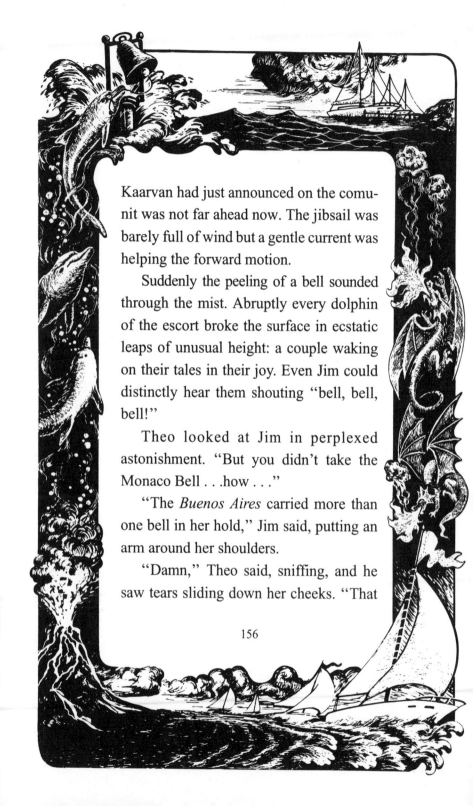

Kaarvan had just announced on the comunit was not far ahead now. The jibsail was
barely full of wind but a gentle current was
helping the forward motion.

Suddenly the peeling of a bell sounded
through the mist. Abruptly every dolphin
of the escort broke the surface in ecstatic
leaps of unusual height: a couple waking
on their tales in their joy. Even Jim could
distinctly hear them shouting "bell, bell,
bell!"

Theo looked at Jim in perplexed
astonishment. "But you didn't take the
Monaco Bell . . .how . . ."

"The *Buenos Aires* carried more than
one bell in her hold," Jim said, putting an
arm around her shoulders.

"Damn," Theo said, sniffing, and he
saw tears sliding down her cheeks. "That

156

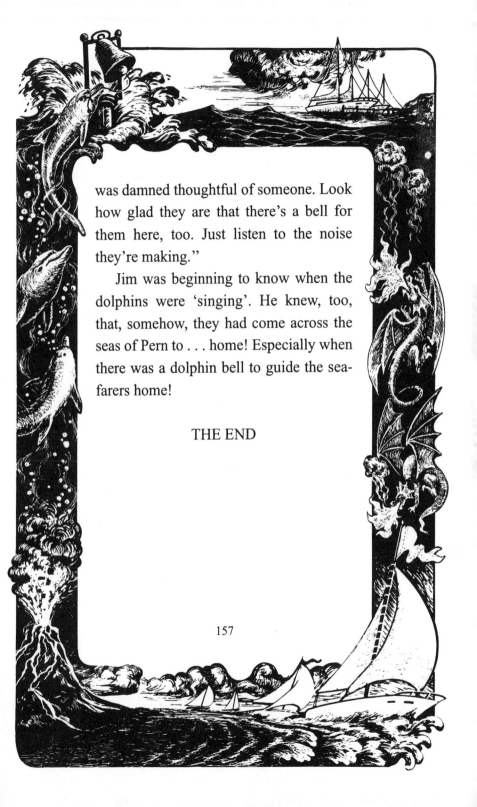

was damned thoughtful of someone. Look how glad they are that there's a bell for them here, too. Just listen to the noise they're making."

Jim was beginning to know when the dolphins were 'singing'. He knew, too, that, somehow, they had come across the seas of Pern to . . . home! Especially when there was a dolphin bell to guide the seafarers home!

THE END

## ABOUT THE AUTHOR

Anne McCaffrey is the most successful woman writer of commercial science fiction ever, with more than 14 million books sold—in English alone. Her novel *All the Weyrs of Pern* appeared on every single best seller list for weeks, including the *New York Times*—just like the novel before it, and the novel before that, and every science fiction novel of hers for the past decade. Ms. McCaffrey makes her home at Dragonhold-Underhill in Ireland.